"*I shouldn't have come here.*"

"No, you shouldn't. I'm not a welfare agency, Mike."

Mike's heart was breaking, shattering. "No, you're not a welfare agency. You're a ruthless, callous, coldhearted beast. I hope your venture fails."

Something ugly blazed into life in his eyes. "It won't," he said softly. "I don't accept failure."

Drawing a deep, painful breath, Mike turned toward the door. "I knew you were despicable," she said viciously, "but I didn't know just how bad!"

His smile showed strong white teeth. "And you haven't even seen me when I've been trying," he said, mocking her. "Given half a chance, I can be much worse than that."

D0048308

ROBYN DONALD lives in northern New Zealand with her husband and a Corgi dog. They love the outdoors and particularly enjoy sailing and stargazing on warm nights. Robyn doesn't remember being taught to read, but rates reading as one of her greatest pleasures, if not a vice. She finds writing intensely rewarding and is continually surprised by the way her characters develop independent lives of their own.

Books by Robyn Donald

HARLEQUIN PRESENTS PLUS
1639—PAGAN SURRENDER

HARLEQUIN PRESENTS
1464—SOME KIND OF MADNESS
1505—STORM OVER PARADISE
1537—THE GOLDEN MASK
1565—ONCE BITTEN, TWICE SHY
1577—THE STONE PRINCESS
1611—SUCH DARK MAGIC
1666—PARADISE LOST

Don't miss any of our special offers. Write to us at the following address for information on our newest releases.

Harlequin Reader Service
U.S.: 3010 Walden Ave., P.O. Box 1325, Buffalo, NY 14269
Canadian: P.O. Box 609, Fort Erie, Ont. L2A 5X3

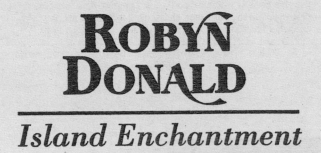

ROBYN DONALD

Island Enchantment

Harlequin Books

TORONTO • NEW YORK • LONDON
AMSTERDAM • PARIS • SYDNEY • HAMBURG
STOCKHOLM • ATHENS • TOKYO • MILAN
MADRID • WARSAW • BUDAPEST • AUCKLAND

ISBN 0-373-11699-3

ISLAND ENCHANTMENT

Copyright © 1993 by Robyn Donald.

CHAPTER ONE

STUDIOUSLY not looking at the tallest man in the group, Mike Christopher asked, 'Are you all going to Far Winds Hotel?'

There was a chorus of affirmatives in a variety of languages. The tall man with the handsome face and proud bearing didn't move. A sharp stab of foreboding emphasised the odd awareness that had gripped her when she had noticed that she was the object of his intent, unnerving regard. In a brusque voice Mike said, 'OK, let's go, then.'

Bending, she picked up a carton of groceries and loaded it on to the little ferry. As usual, most of the passengers began hastily to hoist their packs and cases on to the *Celeste*. Mike's height of five feet two gave people the wrong idea. Although she looked fragile, hard work and sport had given her muscles instead of smooth slenderness, so she was strong enough to deal with most luggage that came her way. Not that she ever got much of a chance; men seemed to find it unbearable to watch her heave boxes and cartons around.

Macho protectiveness, she thought, reaching out towards the last, obviously expensive suitcase. Men also tended to look slightly sideways when they were ferried by a woman around the Bay of Islands, watching surreptitiously until they were sure she could handle the craft.

'I'll do it.' A lean hand took the case from her grasp.

Looking up, Mike relinquished it with a smile that barely made it past the first instinctive curve of her mouth. The deep voice and crisp, educated accent belonged to the man who had watched with hooded eyes

5

beneath dark winged brows when she had run down the wharf.

Something about that narrowed scrutiny pulled Mike's skin taut in an age-old response to danger. Which was stupid, because what danger could he be to her?

If he wanted a holiday romance he would have to find it among the other, mainly youthful guests at Far Winds. Judging by the eager sideways appraisals he was getting from the three women in the group, he wouldn't have to look far.

Mike was not in the market.

'Some men,' her mother had warned, 'see the staff as an added extra.'

Men like your father.

A few uncomfortable experiences during the next two or three years had reinforced her mother's cynical statement, so she had developed, and always been careful to maintain, a pleasant yet impersonal front when dealing with the men who came to Far Winds.

Not, she thought wryly as she flipped the rope off the bollard and swung into the wheel-house, that the tall, dark man looked at all susceptible. In spite of his good looks, the word that sprang to mind when she looked at him was 'tough'.

With the skill of long experience she eased the little ferry away from the wharf. A puff of wind tousled her short black hair, sending one curly strand across pale silver-blue eyes. It had been hot all day, and in spite of the thin material of her shirt she could feel sweat trickling down her backbone.

Still, that was summer in the north of New Zealand, and Mike was accustomed to it. She had been born in the hospital a few miles inland, had lived in the Bay of Islands for the twenty years of her life, and on Far Winds Island for the last twelve. Linda Christopher had been the housekeeper at the hotel until she had died four years ago; Mike still lived in the quarters she had shared with her mother, a tiny cottage separated from the white beach by a hedge of hibiscus bushes.

Turning the wheel a trifle so that she was on course for Russell, she increased speed.

Almost immediately a man came up to the narrow deck outside the wheel-house door. Mike knew who he was without even seeing his face. It was as though the dark stranger with the spare, hawk-like features could reach her in unknown, esoteric ways, probing through the prison of flesh to contact her directly, mind to mind. Even as she scoffed at her unusual whimsy, a slow, breaking excitement swept through her, drying her mouth and making her hands clench a moment on the wheel.

She slid an involuntary glance in his direction. He was, she thought, trying hard to be objective, more than the sum of his parts; he was saved from bland handsomeness by a forceful assurance that set off muted warning sirens all through her. Against the glittering blue of the sea his profile was strikingly resolute, from the high forehead down the straight nose to the square angularity of his chin. In his mid-twenties, he was compellingly attractive, and well aware of it.

She didn't have time to drag her eyes away before he turned. Dark lashes as long and thick as a child's lifted as he returned her survey with unhurried, systematic thoroughness.

Hot with embarrassment and anger, Mike gave him a stiff smile. Immediately she could have kicked herself, for he took it as an invitation. Moving with a casual grace that didn't alter as the little craft bucked its way across the wake of a large cruiser going much too fast for the enclosed waters of the Bay, he stepped into the wheel-house. He knew his way around boats.

'Hello,' he said, and smiled. It was like a flare of white heat, charming, powerfully appreciative. And he understood its effect on women; he used that smile like a weapon.

Mike's body sprang to life. Alarmed and bewildered by her inability to control her reactions, she managed a cool nod. 'Hello. You're not actually supposed to come in here.'

'No?' His smile narrowed. 'Are you going to throw me out?'

She couldn't stop the quick flick of her glance. For all his height and breadth he possessed a smooth athlete's poise, and when he changed position his muscles flexed and coiled beneath bronzed skin in a smooth, effortless motion that promised strength to go with his size.

'No,' she said after a taut second. 'Just don't sue us if I hit anything.'

'I don't think my conversation's interesting enough to put you off that much.'

He was laughing at her, eyes blue as the sheen on an old sword glinting through his dark lashes.

Heat warmed Mike's olive skin, touched her cheekbones with a dusky, evanescant glow. Hastily assuming the capable, friendly yet detached air that served her so well in her dealings with the public, she said, 'It doesn't really matter. We're not a ferry for hire. Far Winds Hotel uses the *Celeste* to take our guests around the Bay. That's why we're going to Russell now; I dropped off four people this morning to have a look around.'

Yes, she sounded fully in control. But that prickle of awareness still raked across her nerves. The brilliant golden and blue light, the glitter of the water and the smooth, muscular shapes of the hills, their tawny slopes shaded by darkly olive gullies, hit her with an almost physical impact.

Don't be an idiot, she scolded herself. You've seen handsome men before. Turned them down, too, without a single regret. What's so different about this one?

Something set him apart from those others, something that pierced the barriers she had considered impregnable and homed on to a primitive, receptive weakness deep inside her.

So, she decided edgily, she was attracted to him. Well, it had to happen sooner or later. She'd just have to make sure it didn't get out of hand.

Assuming that he gave her any encouragement, which was unlikely. Men like this one could have their pick of women. And something about him, some aura of experience, of inherent knowledge, warned her that he was no innocent where the opposite sex was concerned.

She concentrated on guiding the ferry between the two small islands off Paihia, then headed towards Russell on its hilly little peninsula, handling the craft with an effortless skill that revealed just how familiar she was with boats. And all the time the dark stranger watched her.

Mike pretended to be unaffected by his speculative survey, but it sent off more tiny explosions beneath her skin, at once exciting and upsetting.

She fixed her clear, pale blue gaze on the small town that took its burden of history lightly. In spite of the holiday-makers jostling along the waterfront and the wharf, Russell had its own raffish charm. Basically a working town, it was characterised by an honest, sometimes shabby forthrightness that added depth to the transcendent beauty of its setting, making it somehow more substantial than any of the more tinselly tourist destinations. Mike had lived there until she was eight, and she loved it.

'Can we see Far Winds from here?'

'Not yet,' she said, wondering why his textured voice did such strange things to her stomach and legs. 'It's around the end of Tapeka Point.'

'Where's that?'

Mike indicated the point with its beach and cluster of houses. 'Over there.'

Turning the wheel a fraction to avoid a windsurfer who displayed even more than was normal of that breed's famed insouciance, she concentrated on manoeuvering her way through the returning pleasure boats and yachts into Kororareka Bay.

The daytime crush on the wharf had dissipated, but the anchorage was filling fast with craft. It was almost dusk, and the sweet hush that evening brought was tinged with a glowing pink harbinger of the sunset.

The handsome stranger said, 'I'll do the ropes.'

'No, it's all right,' she said swiftly.

'I know how to.'

He looked as though there was very little he didn't know how to do, and do well. Producing what she hoped to be a calm smile, Mike explained, 'I can't let you, I'm afraid; it's against regulations. Don't worry; I've done it a thousand times.'

He said nothing, but she wondered at the way his mouth hardened. Perhaps he was the sort of unregenerate chauvinist who didn't believe women were capable of anything beyond their traditional chores in the kitchen and house.

However, he didn't try to interfere. It took only a few minutes to load the four who waited for them, and then they were once more on their way.

Far Winds was one of the closest islands to the mainland so it didn't take long to reach, even in the *Celeste*, which was slow and prone to breakdowns at the most awkward of moments.

Her finger-nails, short and still slightly grubby, were mute evidence of that. That morning the engine had conked out just as she had been about to take three divers out to Cape Brett, and she'd had to get a part from Paihia out on the water taxi before they could go.

Far Winds Hotel needed a big injection of capital, but the owner didn't seem to be much concerned about the slow deterioration of the complex. A few years before, when guests complained, he'd lowered the tariffs, and eventually, inevitably, they had lost their AA ranking, so that now, instead of being the premier resort in the

Bay of Islands, Far Winds was little more than a backpackers' lodge run with a skeleton staff.

And a proprietor who was drinking more than he should.

Frowning, Mike turned the bow towards Tapeka. 'We'll see Far Winds in a moment,' she said. The man beside her made her feel so small, she thought confusedly, trying to dampen down the unexpected incandescence of pleasure that swept through her body and turned her brain to mush when he smiled.

'Is that it?' he asked, nodding at the island which was rapidly appearing around the point.

His crisp voice with its unusual timbre, masculine and forceful, reverberated through Mike. Control tightened her vocal chords to such an extent that the words came out in a flat monotone. 'Yes, that's it.'

Those hard eyes scanned the island, keen and unwavering. 'The hotel doesn't look very big.'

Mike's shoulders moved defensively. 'It's not a flash modern resort. If that's what you thought you were coming to, you're going to be disappointed.'

Brows lifting in silent surprise, he sent her a slanted glance. Horrified by the impulse that made her snap that sentence out, and mindful too late that it was her job to keep the guests happy, Mike went on in a more conciliatory tone, 'It's more of a lodge, really. Since the hotel at Otehei Bay burned down, Far Winds is the only island with a hotel on it in the Bay of Islands.'

'A lodge? That's not what the brochure says.' His tone was idle. Without taking his eyes off the rapidly approaching island, he asked, 'Has it changed hands recently?'

Mike's expression settled into bleakness. She had been after Harry to change the brochures, with a complete lack of success.

'They're perfectly all right,' he said whenever she protested. 'They're only three years old. Nobody's complained, have they?'

'Not yet. And they're six years out of date, not three!'
The brochures had been printed when Far Winds had
some pretensions to being a resort.

Aloud, she said now, 'No, but we've changed with the
changes in tourist patterns. Many of our visitors are far
more interested in actually seeing the Bay than lying
about on the beach. They're young and cosmopolitan,
and they like to be active. We do fishing and abseiling,
diving and dolphin watching, and at the right time of
the year we go out to watch the humpback whales on
their trip back to the Antarctic.'

'Do you run all the activities yourself?'

'Not all of them,' she said neutrally. Very few, in fact.
Once they had, but Harry had been unable to keep up
the maintenance of the necessary craft, so they'd had to
cut back. Firms in Paihia and Russell had taken up the
slack.

It was a vicious spiral, but Harry just didn't seem to
care any more.

The waters in the channel had been whipped up slightly
by the wind. Mike concentrated on keeping the craft on
an even keel so that her passengers weren't splashed by
the occasional spray. Some tourists were fussy about
getting wet.

The man beside her was once more scrutinising the
island, those dark eyes probing each hill and valley. No
expression showed on the strongly etched features.
Mike's eyes drifted across wide shoulders, uncon-
sciously registering the cut and quality of his clothes.
Made for him, she'd guarantee. He'd be horribly out of
place at the hotel; his clothes, his manner, his air, all
breathed of money and sophistication, a worldliness that
was not so much based on experience as inborn.

This man knew exactly what he was doing, and why;
therefore he knew what he was going to. So what was
he doing here?

Clad in cotton trousers and a polo shirt, he was
perhaps a trifle overdressed—almost everyone else on

the boat was wearing shorts and a skimpy T-shirt—but nobody would notice that. He was a man who stood out, a man of potent, natural charisma, a man who expected the best the world had to offer. Not the sort of man who enjoyed slightly sleazy, run-down hotels like Far Winds.

A chill of uneasiness shivered across her skin. Mike lifted an arm and pointed ahead. 'You can see the wharf now.'

'Yes. Both those hills are part of the island, are they?'

'Yes. They look like separate islands, don't they? But they're joined by a long sand-spit. On the map Far Winds looks like a dumb-bell with one end much bigger than the other.'

'The brochure said something about lagoons. How many are there?'

'Three. Two of them almost eat through the spit, like bites into a slice of cheese.'

'Can you take a boat in?'

'Only a dinghy. They're far too shallow for anything else, and the entrances are dangerous and rocky. They're superb for snorkelling and swimming.' Thank heavens they were almost there. As she cut the engine she said lamely, 'Well, this is it.'

He eyed the wharf. 'It doesn't look safe,' he commented.

In a tone that was too sharp she retorted, 'It's been checked and certified.'

His gaze roamed across her indignant face. A sardonic smile didn't soften his hard mouth. 'Presumably by the proprietor's brother.' It was said lightly, but she heard the cynicism behind it.

Held prisoner by those amazing eyes, Mike was dazed by a strange sense of recognition, as though she knew him—or had been waiting for him all her life. In a voice that wobbled slightly, she said, 'No. Harry doesn't cheat. Anyway, that's not the way things are done here. The wharf's safe.'

'Harry is the owner, I assume.'

'Yes. Harry Sinclair,' she said curtly. She took the *Celeste* in, and by the time she had tied her up she had regained a little of her composure.

Scrambling up on to the wharf, she cast an exasperated glance towards the hotel. Where the hell was Sean, porter and handyman and gardener? He should have been there to meet them, but, as was happening more and more frequently, there was no sign of him.

Still, the guests didn't seem to mind. They picked up their gear from the boat and dumped it on to the trolley, and then helped her with the groceries.

Mike checked to make sure nothing was left on the boat. That done, she positioned herself behind the trolley and began to push. Reluctantly, the slowly turning wheels screamed harshly on the rusting rails.

Instantly an abrupt voice said, 'Here, I'll do that.' It was the dark stranger.

Muscles bunching beneath the knit fabric of his shirt, he pushed. The trolley eased away down the tracks, wailing in a particularly tooth-juddering fashion all the while. As soon as the other men realised what he was doing they went to help him, but the two women who exchanged glances didn't look at them; their avid eyes lingered only on the tall New Zealander.

To her horrified bewilderment, Mike was assailed by a pang of protest so acute that she thought it must glow like neon in her face. Schooling her expression to a stony lack of interest, she walked with the other women along the splintery planks to the end of the wharf.

'Reception's just up the path,' she said, 'in the building behind the tamarisks.'

Oh, she'd tear a strip off Sean, except that when she asked why he hadn't turned up she'd probably discover that he'd been doing something else equally necessary, like getting the generator to work. Equipment was always breaking down; there no longer seemed to be money for anything but the most essential maintenance.

However this group, with the possible exception of the dark stranger, didn't seem to be the complaining kind. All they wanted was a cheap place to stay while they explored the Bay of Islands. Chattering cheerfully, everyone unloaded their luggage and trooped up the path. Everyone except one person, who stood looking down at Mike with a cool interest that made her absurdly self-conscious.

'Do you need something?' she asked rather desperately, bracing herself.

'How old are you?'

Mike's hackles bristled. She knew she looked younger than her twenty years, but he had no right to be so patronising. 'I'm old enough to drive the ferry,' she pointed out, not without relish.

The steely sheen in his eyes was echoed in his voice. 'You have a ticket, I presume?'

'Of course.' Arrogant swine. Most tourists were pleasant enough, but there were the occasional ones who liked to make life hell.

'What's your position here?'

'General dogsbody,' she returned smartly and truthfully. Mike could do almost anything at the hotel, and did, taking over when the cook had her days off, cleaning rooms, waiting behind the bar or at the tables, filling in and making up accounts.

He looked consideringly at her, then the hard features relaxed into that smile that caused a strange softening in her gut. 'My name,' he said, holding out his hand, 'is Guy Lorimer. What's yours?'

'Mike Christopher.' She accepted his handshake with profound reluctance. His hand was firm and cool, and when he touched her little sparks shot up her arm and ignited deep in the pit of her stomach.

'How do you do?' His smile was a miracle, pure charm, lazy, amused, nearly conspiratorial. 'How old *are* you?'

She gave him a wary look. 'Twenty. How old are you?'

His eyes roamed her face in a survey that was not exactly unpleasant, more measuring. He didn't seem annoyed by her near insolence. 'Twenty-six.'

Although he looked about that she would have guessed him to be a lot older than she was. He was certainly much more forceful and self-assured. But then almost anyone in the world was bound to be more sophisticated than a woman who had spent her entire life in the Bay of Islands. Even in New Zealand, a country not exactly noted for its cosmopolitan urbanity, Northland was a backwater.

For the first time in her life Mike wished that she was beautiful and worldly, and had been to university, an ambition she'd had to jettison when her mother had died.

'Well, I'd better go and register, I suppose,' he said. He picked up his suitcase and overnight bag from the trolley and walked beside her up the path. She had to give him credit for his composure. His expression didn't alter as they walked up the uneven path towards the clustered buildings.

The first part of the hotel guests saw were the cabins which Harry, years ago, had decided would look appropriate decorated as grass huts. Strings and tatters of flax fibre still flapped forlornly around the decrepit little structures. Mike intended to get them painted this coming winter, although Harry had been vaguely offhand when she had mentioned it. Still, she was determined. If Harry wouldn't help she'd do it by herself.

Guy Lorimer's face gave nothing away, but Mike looked through those blue eyes and realised that even with the new coat of paint the hotel was more than shabby and seedy; it was downright dilapidated. It looked incongruous, almost sordid in this setting of exquisite beauty. The blue sky beaming down on it and the blue sea lapping at the white beach only succeeded in emphasising the run-down state of the whole complex.

Fighting to keep the chagrin from her tone, Mike said, 'Reception is over here.'

'Thanks.' Guy Lorimer spoke absently, still surveying the buildings with hooded eyes.

Mike wanted to yell, 'Look at me! I'm a woman!'

Shocked and appalled, because never before had she been stung by that imperative urge to assert her femininity, she bit her lip and counted to ten. Her swift, violent reaction to his patent lack of interest frightened her.

In half an hour she was due to help set out the buffet dinner, but reluctantly she waited until he had looked his fill. Guests liked to feel that they were receiving personal attention, and staff who flounced off were not good for the name of the hotel.

But when the silence became oppressive she asked, 'Are you booked in?'

'Yes.'

'Then I'll see you around,' she said awkwardly.

'Oh, yes,' he said, smiling down at her, 'you'll certainly see me around.'

Mike nodded abruptly and left him, heading straight for her little house in its tiny garden. The scent of the three big pines over the back fence mingled with that of the manuka on the hillside to make a perfume that was the essence of summer—tangy, evocative, with a hidden undertone of salt. Sniffing appreciatively, she let herself in. She had just time to wash and change.

But instead of haring into the bathroom she stood for a moment looking down at the photograph of her mother on her dressing-table.

They didn't look much alike; mother and daughter shared the full mouth, and pale blue-grey eyes, but Linda's had been set between pale lashes and brows, whereas Mike's were startling beneath thick black lashes. Linda Christopher had been ethereally fair, with white skin and blonde hair. Mike had her father's Mediterranean colouring and mop of black curls, and in her his stockiness was softened into curves by femininity.

Mike sighed. Her mother had had a wretched life. Linda had told her the full story not long before she died; it had been a holiday romance when her mother was only eighteen, her father a couple of years older. He had left without looking back, and Linda had been too proud to ask for child support. Until Mike was eight they had lived with her grandfather, but after his death Linda had taken the only job she had been able to find where a child was welcome. Harry's wife had died a few months before, and he had needed a housekeeper for the hotel, so they had moved over to the island. To all intents Linda had been happy.

'I wonder if you really were,' Mike said to the calm, pretty face that half smiled out at her. Sighing soundlessly, she put the photograph back on the dresser and went into the bathroom.

'I could eat a horse,' she said half an hour later as she came in through the kitchen door.

Nola, the cook, frowned. 'Didn't you have any lunch again today?'

'No, I was too busy.' Mike peered into the saucepans. 'I did the ferry as well as the diving.'

'Make sure you get a decent meal, then. You're getting too thin.' Casually, Nola sliced through a large tomato. 'A fabulous man registered at Reception just as I was coming back. You must have seen him on the ferry.'

'Yes.' Mike grabbed a plate and began to help herself.

'Is he alone? I suppose not. Usually men like him have an equally fabulous woman with them.'

'Not this one, not unless he left her in Paihia.'

'Then he's gay,' Nola decided.

'He's certainly handsome enough,' Mike told her, smiling a little maliciously. 'He looked like a model, I thought.'

Nola grinned. 'He's probably the best-looking man I've seen in my life, but he did not look like a model, for heaven's sake; he looked—oh, *someone*, know what I mean? I mean, models are pretty; this man looked powerful as well. And definitely heterosexual! He'll make a few hearts flutter!'

'I wonder what a man like that's doing at Far Winds?' Mike said, ladling salad on to her plate. 'Let's face it; we don't appeal to the rich and powerful. They like their creature comforts too much.'

Nola shrugged. 'Who knows? Perhaps he wants peace and quiet.'

'Well, we've got plenty of that. But I bet he'll be on the first ferry out tomorrow morning. He doesn't look the type to fit in here. One of the big motels on the Paihia side would appeal to him much more.'

Later that evening, as Mike talked to the band in the big room off the bar that was both hall and overflow restaurant, she looked up to see Guy Lorimer walk past the door towards the bar. At dinner he sat on the other side of the room and Mike had kept her eyes averted; nevertheless, she had noted the two women who sat at his table, and their purposeful, unsubtle pursuit.

That had hurt. No, it hadn't hurt, it had outraged her. For a searing moment she'd felt as though she had some sort of claim on him, as though he and she had been linked by a primitive love spell and the women who flirted so openly with him were intruders.

If they were, they were determined intruders. They met him as he walked into the bar, smiling, casting fascinated, far from aloof glances at him through downswept lashes.

Mike indulged in a momentary daydream, seeing a hot, crowded floor, and herself in something expensive and wildly flattering, something that made her look four inches taller... This time instead of indifference there would be open appreciation in his brilliant eyes, and a smile would curl that hard, beautiful, uncompromising mouth.

Feelings that were unaccountably raw and scratchy tempered her voice. 'So keep the volume down,' she said shortly, dragging her mind back to the point at issue.

'Ah, come on, Mike...' The band leader smiled winningly at her.

'I know, I know,' she said, mock-sympathy dripping through her voice, 'it'll spoil the music, but how do you know that when you never play at anything under three hundred decibels? The wave of the future, according to our overseas visitors, is softer music that they can actually hear, instead of a blur of sound. Conservation, and all that. So give some thought to their poor endangered eardrums. Tone it down, OK, John? You can let yourselves go sometimes, but not all the time.'

John, who for the purposes of his part-time career as band leader was known as Jon, lifted his eyes to the heavens, but he knew better than to protest further, beyond warning, 'They won't like it.'

Heartlessly, she returned, 'It's up to you to *make* them like it.'

'God, you're a cruel woman.' He gazed into her amused eyes with soulful intensity, then startled her by bending her over his arm and kissing her. Instantly the band erupted into catcalls and applause, mingled with a few shouted suggestions for further activity.

So astonished that she was free by the time she made up her mind to resist, Mike spluttered, 'What in the world was that for?'

'Nothing disturbs you, does it?' Slowly shaking his head, John stepped back and surveyed her with a mournful expression that didn't go with the laughter in his eyes. 'You always were a hard little thing, bossy and practical, with your nose forever in a book even at school. Doesn't go with that soft, lush mouth. I've always wondered what it would be like to kiss you. And it was nice. I liked it. But I can see that nothing world-shaking happened to you. I'm desolated. Shut up, you guys.' He sighed theatrically. 'All right, we'll play quietly, cross my heart. But mark my words, Mike Christopher, some day some man is going to come along and he'll find that touch-me-not air a definite challenge.'

Completely unaffected by this melodramatic prophecy, Mike pulled a face and looked around. The room was now swept and decorated with strobe lights and glitter balls. They weren't new, but in the pulsating, throbbing world of the disco it was impossible to see that the equipment was falling apart. Of course, it could choose that night to give up the ghost completely...

Don't even think about it!

Firmly banishing this ever present fear from her mind, Mike turned to check the arrangements for food. A sudden wave of exhaustion caught her completely by surprise. She yawned, and let her gaze drift sideways into the bar.

Guy Lorimer was surrounded by people, but he was looking straight at Mike. Her tentative smile was frozen by the deliberate way he turned his head away. He must have said something, for his entourage laughed. Mike squashed the sour, elemental tug of jealousy and went on her way, reflecting savagely that it was completely unfair for a man to have enough natural charisma to light New Zealand for a couple of days, and the face of a Greek god, too.

Lord, she was tired. The last thing she wanted to do was dance, but it didn't look as though Harry was going to turn up tonight, so her fatigue and her grey mood had to be ignored.

What was wrong with him? He had been like this for a couple of months now, and, although she had asked as delicately as she could, he refused to talk about it. Speculation had been rife, of course; most of the staff thought it was the imminent prospect of bankruptcy that was causing his moods, and were trying to organise themselves new jobs, with a distinct lack of success so far.

If this was so, then Mike was in trouble. She had no qualifications, no home and no relatives to help her out.

But it was useless to worry about her future just now. She caught a glimpse of herself in a mirror and stopped

to straighten the wide boat neck of her Chinese-blue dress
and adjust the panels of its floating skirt. Her bare, satiny
legs and narrow feet had tanned warmly, setting off both
frock and Chinese-blue sandals. Neither dress nor shoes
were new, but they looked good on her, deepening the
colour of her eyes and redeeming her skin from
sallowness.

'Oh, there you are, Mike.'

She looked up sharply. Harry came ambling around
the corner, a bear of a man with a shaggy, greying beard
and even shaggier hair. As he got closer she realised that
he hadn't been drinking, and relief lightened the strain
on her small face.

'Mike, have you seen a letter from England?'

'England? No, I don't think we've had a letter from
England recently.'

His bushy brows twitched together. 'It's about the
lease,' he said.

Mike nodded, understanding. The island was owned
by a family trust in England.

'It's time to renew it,' he said fretfully, looking around
as though the letter had been hidden near by. 'They want
some enormous increase, but I told them that the present
economic situation means that's ridiculous. After all,
inflation is practically zero now. There's no need to up
the rent.'

Mike nodded again.

'Well, it doesn't matter. Don't you go worrying about
it; it'll turn up.' A loud burst of music brought his head
around. He stared at the door as though it had suddenly
gone insane, then said heavily, 'Oh, yes. It's the dance
tonight, isn't it? Have fun.'

'I hope so,' she said, amazed that he didn't react to
her dry tone.

He stood irresolute for a moment, then turned and
shambled back towards his flat. Frowning, Mike watched
until he had disappeared before heading purposefully
towards the restaurant.

Ten minutes later she went through to the courtyard at the back where the pool sparkled an unnatural blue in the last rays of the sun. People were still swimming, but more were taking advantage of summer's long evening to walk along the beach, most of them, she noted with wry amusement as she straightened chairs and swiftly collected glasses, hand in hand. Judging by the laughter that drifted up from the sands, they all seemed imbued with that particular carefree light-heartedness that marked holidays.

Mike envied them. It was not a nasty, niggling 'why not me?' envy, but a kind of cosmic yearning, a longing for the fresh, open joy of youth. When her mother had died Mike's innocent conviction that the world was hers, that happiness was her birthright, had been shattered. She had discovered in the cruellest possible way that life could be horribly unfair.

Still, it was useless wallowing in self-pity; reaching down, she picked up another glass.

It turned out to be a good night. The guests had come prepared to enjoy themselves, and enjoy themselves they did. The band was loud, but not deafening, and showed a nice judgement of the crowd by alternating frenetic rock and boogie numbers with slower items, the occasional old-fashioned maxina or veleta or three-step, but mostly waltzes and foxtrots which even the most self-conscious dancers were prepared to try.

The heat brought colour to Mike's cheeks, and she gave herself up to dancing and a little light flirtation, using her long lashes to good effect. By now she was a past master at chatting to people, flattering them with her interest without making herself seem available.

Periodically she glanced towards the door, embarrassed and irritated because she was looking for Guy Lorimer. Which was ridiculous, because a casual country hop didn't seem his sort of thing.

Towards ten he came, tall and hard-edged, walking with an easy, alert gait that brought a clear-cut image of some graceful, lethal predator. With him were two women, not quite so tall, and elegantly blonde—the two Swedish women who had been on the *Celeste* that afternoon.

Mike struggled to calm her suddenly turbulent reactions. It didn't matter a bit to her—she didn't even like the man, and certainly she had no intention of competing for his attention—but in spite of that her heart was going haywire and her skin was hot and sensitive.

The band struck up a waltz, and almost immediately she was whisked on to the floor by a tall young American who seemed to think it was a different dance entirely. After a few badly timed steps he said in his lazy, cheerful drawl, 'We're in trouble here.'

'No, it's easy.' Smiling, ever smiling, Mike gave him a rapid lesson, and by the time the music stopped he was dancing like someone from old Vienna, spinning her in circles that came to a finish right next to Guy Lorimer.

Mike's heart stopped. As though Mike's jagged awareness communicated itself to him his lashes flicked up, and for a moment she was held captive by the blue glimmer of his gaze.

His half-puzzled look infuriated her. A devilish impulse stirred her into sending him a sideways, taunting, glittery smile as she turned her back to go off the floor.

Ten minutes later she couldn't see him in the room at all. Good, she told herself. The moment she had done it she had regretted that smile. She wasn't in the habit of being provocative.

She was laughing with the American, a glass of orange juice in her hand, when they announced the next set. Rock and roll this time.

When Guy said from behind her, 'May I have this dance?' her pulses went into overdrive.

Slowly she turned. He was smiling, and that smile was pure challenge.

It was answered by something rash and wild that sprang to life within Mike. Meeting the blue gauntlet of his gaze, alert and amused and vital, she felt an answering challenge expand to fill her with a vivid courage.

'Yes, of course,' she said, draining her orange juice.

His glance lingered on the sheen of juice on her mouth. Uneasily, she licked it off, and saw with surprise his eyes narrow a second. His smile altered, became imbued with a quality she didn't understand, and he held out his hand.

After a smile and a few laughing words to the American, Mike obeyed the command. Streaks of sensation, sharp and intoxicating, ran up her arm. Hastily repressing her instinctive desire to rub the skin, she went with Guy out on to the floor.

He took her into his arms, smiling down at her, his tall, lithe body moving with the assurance that came from complete confidence.

'How are you enjoying your stay so far?' she asked when the silence threatened to stretch too long.

His shoulders lifted slightly. 'It's—interesting.'

Mike was proud of her composure. She smiled. 'Oh, that's good; I'm glad.'

Her voice had just the right sort of tone, the talking-to-tourists pitch that surely hid the erratic thunder of her heart. Dancing with him was having the most alarming effect on her, and she didn't know how to deal with it.

Guy said, 'The island is beautiful. How many beaches are there on it?'

'Seven. One for each day of the week,' Mike told him. 'Each one's named after a day.'

'By someone with a sense of humour. Can you get to them all?'

'Oh, yes, there are tracks.'

'Why don't you show me one tomorrow?'

She didn't believe she'd heard him correctly, and after a stunned pause replied, 'I'm sorry, but I can't; I'm working all day. They're well signposted, though.'

'Some other time, perhaps.' He didn't sound as though he really wanted her to go with him; his voice was conventionally disappointed, but she discerned indifference beneath it. 'How long have you been driving ferries?'

'A couple of years.'

Something gleamed in the blue depths of his eyes. 'I thought you were a schoolgirl when I saw you run down the wharf at Paihia with that carton in your arms.'

So that was why he had watched her so intently! She gave him a glossy smile and said brightly, 'I stopped growing when I was fourteen. It was a definite blow to my ego, believe me.'

'Good things come in small packages, my father used to say.'

Mike said sweetly, 'Yes, I've been told that, too. It's always sounded utterly patronising.'

Laughing, he whirled her into a pirouette that led easily into the classic rock and roll steps. Mike had been taught by Harry, who was an expert, so she followed without even thinking about it. Whoever Guy had learned from was equally adept; he danced with skill and a raw energy that surprised her.

Fairly soon the other dancers made a space for them and stood around clapping in time to the music. Mike was not vain but she knew she could dance well, and it was a real pleasure to partner someone as good as Guy.

The band caught fire, and what had been a routine dance number suddenly became an exhibition that ended with Mike, flushed and laughing, being twirled until she was breathless before finally being caught and hugged against him as the music roared to a finish and everyone around them clapped and yelled.

And then it was no longer fun. The laughter died in her throat as she looked helplessly up into eyes that glittered strangely. She tried to react normally, as though the heat and pressure of a man's embrace was a common experience for her. It was difficult, because her breath was stopped in her lungs, and a violent hunger, exquisite, imperative, was stabbing through every nervecell in her body.

'You may be small,' he murmured as he set her away from him, 'but you definitely pack a punch.'

He was flirting with her, yet something beneath the smooth compliment, something deeper and more exciting, worried Mike. Jerking herself a safe distance away, she turned her head so that he couldn't see her face. It was a shock to hear her husky voice say, 'I'm so hot.'

'Do you want to cool down outside?'

For a moment she almost said yes. Temptation purred at her with fierce power, but years of caution stood her in good stead.

'No, I'll just have some orange juice,' she said, and set off for the bar. She told herself that she didn't want him to come with her, but she knew just how hypocritical she was being when she felt his hand at her waist, guiding her through the crowd.

'Mike,' he said, a note of laughter in his voice. When she looked up enquiringly he said, 'It's a strange name for a girl.'

CHAPTER TWO

MIKE shrugged. 'It's better than Michaela. But then anything's better than Michaela.'

'Michaela? Well, it's certainly different.'

Mike laughed. 'It's longer than I am!'

'Were you named after someone?'

'My father.'

She hoped her withdrawal was imperceptible, but those shrewd eyes noticed. However, he didn't probe, and she certainly wasn't going to tell him that when she had been named her mother had still hoped the man who'd betrayed her would come back. Mike had grown up watching that hope fade and die.

At the bar Guy stood back, waiting his turn. Ignoring the other man who had reached the bar just before them, Nola dimpled and smiled and asked him for his order. Guy nodded at the man beside him and said, 'He's first.'

The young man smiled. Somewhat flustered, Nola dealt with his order before switching her bemused eyes to Guy.

Amazing. Nola was behind the bar because she was tough enough to tell any visiting yachtie that he'd had too much to drink, and make it stick. Yet she crumpled under a touch of charm.

Mike understood. It was like having a million-watt light turned on you, and only you. The man was dangerous. When he looked at her like that she could almost imagine that no other woman meant anything to him.

Of course, even though she hadn't experienced it before, she knew what was happening to her. Mike Christopher, that byword for inaccessibility, was suffering from her first bout of physical attraction.

28

Probably its potency was due to the fact that she was a late starter.

She could feel a fizzing in her blood, as though she'd drunk too much champagne, and her gaze had a disconcerting tendency to drift upwards and linger on the arrogant angles of his face, be snared by the burning blue depths of his.

A couple of youths down the back of the hall let out wild yells. The raucous noise broke the spell. 'Thank you,' Mike said faintly, and swallowed some of the cold liquid, relishing the sweetness and flavour.

'You have the most amazing eyes,' he said. 'So pale, exactly halfway between grey and blue, silvery and translucent. I don't think I've ever seen eyes that colour before.'

His words sizzled through her nerve-ends, but she recognised the approach of a practised flirt. Her left eyebrow lifted a fraction, an elegant black question mark. 'Thank you,' she said politely. 'Yours are an unusual colour, too.'

He grinned. 'I was not spinning you a line. Finish your drink and we'll dance again.'

This time it was a foxtrot. Mike went into his arms with reservations that didn't last much beyond the first few bars. He danced like a dream, her mother had said once about her father. Now Mike knew what she meant, understanding for the first time just how seductive male grace could be. Guy's arm about her, and the way he took command of her responses, the faint, elusive scent of his masculinity, a clean saltiness shot through with a hint of musk that owed nothing to aftershave, sent icy tremors through every cell in her body.

Lost in a myriad sensory signals, all of them new and astonishing, she followed him blindly. His arm tightened across her back as he swung her into a pirouette, a long leg between hers in sudden, shocking intimacy. Something torrid and primitive and unrestrained flamed into life in the pit of Mike's stomach. She tensed, trying

to pull away, but his arm didn't slacken, so she had to
follow while her inner turmoil flamed out of control,
setting logic and thought alight, breaching the defences
of a lifetime.

By the time the dance ended she knew she had to get
away from him. Smiling, so that he wouldn't realise how
vulnerable she was, she said lightly, 'That was fun, but
I'd better——'

Another ruction at the back of the hall whipped her
head around. Something shifted, blurred, in Mike's
vision. Instantly alert, moving with speed and razor-sharp
reactions, Guy stepped in front of her.

'Let me past!' she said, pushing at him.

'You can't go down there.' His hand on her arm was
just short of painful. 'A couple of idiots are fighting.'

'Guy, that's my job; that's why I'm here.'

He hesitated, but when she pulled away from him, her
small squared-off chin set in determination, he didn't
try to stop her. Nevertheless he was right beside her when
she reached the brawling pair, whose flushed cheeks and
glittering eyes made it obvious that the fight was fuelled
by alcohol.

Mike knew them both; they had come over from
Russell. Red-faced and grunting as they traded blows,
few of which connected, they were too drunk for an
appeal to their better instincts.

Thinking quickly, Mike asked the woman next to her,
'Is that straight orange juice? No spirits?'

'Just orange juice,' she said hesitantly.

'May I have it?' The woman handed it over and in a
single smooth motion Mike threw the cold juice at the
one who seemed to be winning.

It hit him fair in the middle of his face. Gasping, he
instinctively jerked, and his punch landed harmlessly in
mid-air. The other turned around belligerently, swearing,
his fists clenching as he tried to fathom out who had
thrown the liquid.

'That will do,' Mike said sharply. 'Get out.'

There was a sudden hush as people realised what was happening. From beside her, Guy said quietly, 'You'd better do as she says.'

'Says who?' the older one snarled, but he took a step back.

Mike's voice was crisp and icy and confident. 'I say, Simon Armstrong.'

'And so,' said Guy, something in his tone electrifying the air, 'do I.'

From the corner of her eyes Mike saw a couple of the more husky guests take up positions, while Sean and one of the housemaids were forging their way through the crowd.

'Come on,' she commanded. 'Everyone's staring.'

'Oh, a'right,' Simon Armstrong said thickly, the drunken antagonism of a moment ago softening rapidly into sheepishness. 'C'on, Dirk, let's get outa here.'

'Thank you,' Mike said to the woman whose orange juice she had commandeered. 'Tell Nola at the bar what happened, and she'll get you another drink.' She smiled professionally at Guy. 'And thank you, too.'

She turned away.

'Where do you think you're going?' Guy demanded.

She gave him a genuinely bewildered look. 'I'm going to find out where those kids got their booze, then I'm taking them back to Russell.'

'You are not.'

She stared at him. Up on the dais the band struck up a tune. Everyone lost interest in the fight and began to look around for partners. Simon and Dirk wandered through the door and out into the scented night.

Mike said steadily, 'I'm not going to have them stumbling around the hotel. They're drunk enough to find trouble without looking for it. Thank you for your help, but——'

'Where the hell is the owner, or the manager?' he demanded roughly. 'Or the bloody porter, come to that!

It's intolerable that a kid like you should have to deal with situations like this.'

Mike's chin came up and her eyes were frozen chips as she replied, 'Don't take my size as any indication of my ability to cope! I can deal with——'

'Don't be a fool! What if they turn nasty?'

'They won't.'

'Where is the owner?' Guy demanded relentlessly, his expression revealing as much pugnacity as the boys' had a moment ago, only this was a controlled aggression, dominated by an acute intelligence and subject to his will.

'He's not able to help,' Mike snapped back.

'Why not?'

Gulping enough oxygen to ease her jumping nerves, she drew a deep breath. 'I'm not going to bandy words with you.' She strode outside, her stiff shoulders and back defying him to stop her.

Guy didn't try, but from immediately behind came his voice, soft and deadly. 'What makes you think you can cope with them?'

'They're harmless.' She stopped and directed a determined glance at his silhouette, big and dominating against the lights of the hotel. 'Thank you for helping, but really, it's all right now. They're just a couple of stupid boys I've known all their lives.'

He snorted and kept on coming. Angry, feeling as though she had broken her knuckles against a totally unyielding wall, Mike wavered, then turned away. The two boys were leaning against a stone wall, arguing in slurred voices.

'Oh, shut up, both of you,' Mike interrupted without ceremony. 'Where did you get your booze from?'

They goggled at her. 'Aw, come on, Mike, don't be like that,' Simon said after a moment. 'We're shorry; it was all just a bit of fun, washn't it, Dirk?'

Dirk nodded enthusiastically, his eyes sliding from Mike's furious face to that of the man with her. 'He's me mate,' he offered, as though it explained everything.

'Simon,' she said forcefully, 'where did you get that beer?'

'We brought it with us.' He glowered at her. 'You won't sell it to us so we had to bring it here.'

'How did you get over?'

Both boys looked at each other, until Simon said reluctantly, 'We hitched a ride with Jordan Phillips. We were going to sh-sleep on the beach then go back on the ferry in the morning.'

Mike said evenly, 'All right. I'll take you back to Tapeka Point. I've got enough to worry about without wondering whether you two idiots have fallen into the water and drowned yourselves.'

After a moment for this to sink in, Dirk said diffidently, 'I don't live at Tapeka Point. Come to think of it, Simon doesn't, too. Either, I mean.'

'Tough. You might sober up enough on the walk home for your fathers not to ground you,' Mike retorted heartlessly. She turned to look at Guy Lorimer. 'Would you mind very much keeping an eye on them until I get back?'

'Not in the least.' The sudden radiance of the moon limned his face in silver; he looked older and harsher—a warrior from an antique coin, she thought fancifully as she turned away.

Ten minutes later she was back. Sean and a couple of the other workers had been organised into a temporary vigilante group; it was the best she could do in the circumstances. Responsibility weighed heavily on her shoulders. She had to battle an aching weariness that threatened to swamp her sense of humour entirely. Mixed with it was chagrin. She had wanted Guy Lorimer to think well of her, and of Far Winds, and now he must be convinced the place was rough and raw and provincial.

The boys, she noted as she came towards the small, silent group, were almost asleep. Guy's tall, lean figure stood a little apart. Hands thrust into his pockets, he was staring out to sea.

'Come on, guys,' she said as she came up. 'Time to go.'

'You going to maroon him at Tapeka Point, too?' Simon asked artlessly, staring with owlish eyes at Guy.

'No.' Mike looked up into a dark, impassive face, her glance lingering a furtive second on the moonlit angles and planes, the hard male contours. 'Thank you,' she said, infusing her tone with politeness. 'You've been very helpful, but I can manage now.'

His teeth flashed white in the moonlight. 'I'll come with you,' he said deliberately. 'I like boating at night.'

And he wouldn't be persuaded otherwise. Trailed by the boys, both listening interestedly, Mike argued all the way to the wharf, finally giving up when she realised that she was faced with a resolution stronger than her own. For some reason Guy Lorimer was going with her, and there was nothing she could do about it.

Face set mutinously, she settled them into the run-about and took off with quite unnecessary speed, trying to shake off the sudden radiant pleasure that mingled with her irritation.

True to her word, she put the boys off at Tapeka Point beach. The cool air whipping past their faces had sobered them somewhat, so she wasn't worried about their safety. Nevertheless she watched until they were safely ashore and had set off up the road towards Russell.

'Do you have much of that sort of thing?' Guy asked as they moved quietly out of the bay.

She shrugged. 'No. We've got a reputation for being tough. They know they can't buy alcohol if they're under age, and we don't encourage guests from off the island. Most of those who do come are well-behaved. Those two were just stupid and feeling their oats. I doubt very much whether they'll try it again.'

'Hmm. What would you do if anyone got dangerously drunk?'

'Harry's quite capable of dealing with them.'

'Not at the moment, it appears,' he pointed out.

Harassed, torn between telling him to mind his own business and the duty she owed to a guest, moreover a guest who had done her a good turn, Mike said obstinately, 'There are plenty of us to cope, as we did tonight.'

And pushed the lever out, effectively preventing any further conversation as they headed back to Far Winds.

It was a magnificent night. The moon picked out the outlines of hills and islands in a glittering wash, glamorising an already poignantly beautiful scene. They should have been sailing, Mike thought as the little craft skipped across the water, the sound of its engine intrusive in the black and silver nocturne. They should have been slipping silently through the moon-dappled sea with ghostly silver sails and nothing but the faint murmur of the water against the hull to keep them company.

Very aware of the man beside her, she kept her eyes resolutely fixed to the front. Even though she knew what was happening, the strength of her reactions frightened her. Thank heavens he wasn't going to be around for long. He had booked in for only a week. Nothing earth-shattering could happen in seven days. You certainly couldn't fall in love in that time.

The thought should have comforted her, but she suspected that where Guy was concerned the usual and normal didn't apply.

They were halfway back when the outboard motor sputtered and, as Mike cursed, died. 'What now?' she moaned, fiddling with the controls.

Nothing worked. She expected Guy to try to take over, but he didn't move or say a word until she gave in and looked at him in mute appeal.

Then, and only then, in a voice so dry it made chills sprint up her spine, he said, 'Is there any petrol in it?'

There wasn't. For a bitter second Mike closed her eyes, biting back the diatribe that tried to escape. It was Sean's duty to top up the engine; however, it was no use railing furiously at him now.

'Can we row home?' Guy asked.

She cast a glance over the side. The faint chuckle and splash of the current warned her that the tide was setting past them. 'Not really,' she said quietly. 'The tide's against us. It would be better to anchor and wait until someone misses us.' If they did. 'I'm so sorry,' she finished inadequately.

He smiled. 'My grandfather taught me early on that what can't be cured has to be endured,' he said, picking up the anchor and throwing it over in a powerful movement. 'Tell me why a twenty-year-old girl is running a resort almost single-handed. Where is this elusive Harry?'

She hesitated, then admitted, 'He's not well.'

'I see.' His voice was remote. 'So how do you come to be running the place?'

'I know what to do.'

'How? I gather you're not holiday staff.'

'No, I've lived on Far Winds for years.' The anchor caught and held. Satisfied that they weren't going to drift anywhere, Mike cleated the warp then sat down on the seat, hugging herself. She wasn't cold yet, but her jacket wouldn't keep her warm for very long.

'How long have you been dogsbody?'

She stiffened, but reluctant honesty compelled her to answer, 'Four years. Ever since my mother died.'

'Sixteen is too young to lose your mother,' he said.

She shivered. In a completely different voice he said, 'You're cold. Come and sit here beside me. We might as well share our body heat.'

'Oh—no, I'm perfectly all——'

'Mike,' he interrupted, sounding bored, 'I'm not going to make a pass, or even kiss you. I just don't want you to get hypothermia, and if nobody notices we don't come back that may well happen. Come to think of it, I don't want to come down with exposure myself.'

She might have been able to resist if he hadn't added that last bit. Which, she thought as she slid across the seat, was probably why he had said it. He was astute enough to realise that she wouldn't want to offend a paying guest.

His arm came to rest across her shoulders, warm and somehow reassuringly heavy. Mike's heart-rate increased; she hoped fervently that he couldn't feel the rapid thudding that seemed to shake her body.

'Where did you live before you came across to the island?' he asked.

'At Russell. Mum and I lived with my grandfather in a little house there, one of the miners' cottages from the old manganese mine a few miles away. When that was worked out someone moved the houses to Russell. There are only two left now, both in Watering Bay.'

'So Far Winds is your home.'

She nodded. 'Yes. Grandad left me a section at Long Bay, but it's up a goat track, so it's not worth anything. One day, though, I'll build a house there. You look right out across the islands, out to Cape Brett. It's beautiful.'

'Do you want to do anything else with your life?'

Mike began to shrug, but stopped halfway through when the movement brought her closer to him. 'I'm quite happy,' she said after a moment. 'I love the island; I love the Bay; I enjoy my job.'

'No further ambitions? Or is it a stopgap until you marry?' His voice was lazy and pleasant.

'Marriage is not on the agenda,' she said, yawning.

'You're not ever planning to get married? Or not just yet?'

It was a strangely intimate conversation. Snuggled against him, Mike felt comforted, almost secure. 'I don't know,' she said slowly. 'It's a big step. I've seen some pretty awful marriages at the hotel, and some quite good ones, but the good ones never seem as good as the awful ones are bad.'

'No.' His voice was oddly sombre, although that might have been the way it reverberated through his chest. 'So why are you running Far Winds?'

'I'm not running it,' she said defensively.

'So Harry isn't just a figment of your imagination?' He sounded amused, lightly teasing.

Harry might just as well be, he did so little around the place now, but she wasn't going to tell Guy that. 'Of course he's not,' she said, wondering for the thousandth time just what was wrong with Harry, and whether there was anything she could do to help him.

Guy didn't say anything more, and for long minutes they sat without talking. At once sleepy and wildly, acutely aware, Mike closed her eyes.

'I think we'd be more comfortable if we leaned against the side,' Guy said, and, without giving her a choice, swung around so that his back was supported by the low gunwale. With a swift, steady movement he lifted her so that she lay curled on his lap, her cheek on his chest, his strongly muscled thighs hard beneath her as he stretched his legs along the seat.

'I'm too heavy,' she said hastily, trying to scramble away.

A firm hand kept her in place. 'Nonsense.'

Of course this meant nothing to him—why should it? He was merely keeping them both as snug as possible.

'Do you know anything about the stars?' he asked.

'I know all the constellations, the Southern Cross, that sort of thing. And the planets. Do you?'

'My grandfather has a telescope, a huge old thing. He used to let me lug it out on to the terrace on starry nights. I'll never forget the first time I saw Jupiter's moons. It was a turning-point in my life. For years afterwards I was determined to be an astronomer.'

'What happened?'

His chest lifted as he gave a short laugh. 'Oh, I'm the only grandson so I had to go into the business.'

Had he been bullied into giving up his choice of a career? Mike's eyes traced the arrogant profile, clean-cut, strong against the luminous sky, and lingered on the harsh male set of the jaw. No, this man would not be bullied. He was an interesting mixture—uncompromising, self-contained, yet there was no mistaking the affection in the deep voice when he spoke of his grandfather. It was love that had persuaded him to give up his ambition to be an astronomer.

'What sort of business?' she asked, clenching her jaws to stop another yawn.

'Are you tired? Why don't you just doze off? I imagine you'll be up at the crack of dawn tomorrow morning.'

'Six,' she said, her smile mutating into another yawn. Lapped in security, wrapped in his warmth and the clean, fresh scent of him, his arms around her, the wall of his chest rising and falling rhythmically against her cheek, she slipped into sleep.

And woke to the sound of Guy's voice and the tickle of his breath in her ear. 'Someone's coming, Mike.' At first she thought it was a dream, but when he said a second time, 'Mike, wake up, sweetheart; someone's coming,' she lifted her tousled head and blinked her eyes open.

It was still dark, but the moon was pitched much lower in the sky, and the pale promise of dawn glowed in the east. The quiet putt-putt of a small outboard swivelled her head around.

For a moment she was completely disorientated, but as soon as she realised where she was she scrambled out of Guy's lap, then had to clutch his shoulder to balance on legs that wobbled in the gently rocking boat. Almost immediately the aluminium dinghy going down the passage altered course.

'That's Geoff Dinant,' she told Guy, who was standing beside her. 'He's going fishing.' She shivered in the bracing air. 'Lord,' she said on a note of shock, 'it's almost morning!'

'The days when a woman was irrevocably compromised if she stayed out with a man all night are long gone,' Guy said in an amused voice.

Mike felt a complete fool. 'I was just surprised it was so late,' she said lamely.

Twenty minutes later they were back on the wharf of the sleeping resort, the only lights the muted glow of the lamps along the paths. Mike noted automatically that three bulbs had died and needed to be replaced.

'It's not half-past five yet, anyway,' she said, shivering with reaction and the moist dampness of the morning. The glow in the east had turned into a pure crystal radiance that promised another brilliant golden day. 'Nola would be baking bread if it were.'

'It's just after five.'

Normally steady on her feet, Mike tripped over a hummock of grass. Instantly his hand shot out and closed around hers.

'Careful.'

'My legs haven't woken up yet,' she said on a half-yawn. 'I'm sorry.'

'Why? You couldn't help it.'

She shook her head. 'No, I'm sorry for keeping you out. It shouldn't have happened.'

His laughter was quiet, almost rueful. 'I've always wanted to be a castaway. There wasn't a desert island, but one can't have everything in this life. Don't worry about it. I'm certainly not going to.'

She gave her hand a tentative tug, but he didn't let go. As they walked across the newly mown grass Mike realised that when she was old and grey she would remember walking into the dawn with Guy Lorimer, the perfume of summer jasmine sweet in her nostrils and in the background the soft hush of waves on the beach, a cool, fresh breeze playing about them. And his hand, lean and warm and secure, around hers. A pang of delight so piercing that it hurt transfixed her.

All too soon it was over. Outside the gate to her small house she said shyly, 'You're very kind, but I'm sorry we got stranded.'

His voice, when it came, was a shock. Gone was the camaraderie of the past hours. Aloofly, without pulling any punches, he said, 'You shouldn't be put into such a position. You could have been out there all night. And you certainly shouldn't have to deal with drunks. Drunk men are dangerous. The normal rules don't apply.'

'Oh, come on, Guy; they're only boys and they could barely stand upright.'

'They are still stronger than you.'

Any further protest would sound churlish. After all, he had helped avert what could have been a tricky situation. Reluctantly she admitted, 'Yes, I know. I'm not stupid, though; I don't take chances, and you saw that there was plenty of help at hand. Anyway, we don't get drunks very often.'

'It's just that you're so small,' he said, then laughed, an unpleasant note of irony darkening his voice.

Mike stiffened. She said firmly, 'My size has nothing to do with anything.'

'Put it down to politically unsound vestiges of the past,' he said. 'I know you can deal with almost anything that comes your way, but because you're tiny I feel I should be protecting you.'

'That's insulting,' Mike said without rancour, still trying to quench the excitement that sizzled through her. She had no illusions; his touch might stir up such a torrent of intense response in her that she barely knew how to deal with it, but she didn't do the same to him.

He swung the gate open, lifting it over the tree root in the path that usually stopped it halfway, and walked her up to the narrow veranda. The breeze prowled

through spiky lavender flowers, carrying their faint, refreshing fragrance across the uneven lawn.

'Thank you,' Mike said firmly.

Another smile, made more potent by the first rays of
the sun. 'For nothing. Goodnight, Mike.'

He kissed her hand. That was all, yet it felt as though
lightning had burned away everything but a violent need
that scorched through in a flood of liquid fire. Clenching
her teeth to stop them chattering, Mike almost ran up
the cracked concrete steps. He waited until she had
opened the door; she gave a half-wave of her hand and
disappeared inside.

Only to creep into the sitting-room and watch him
through the faded muslin curtains as he strode down the
path and closed the gate, and went off, whistling softly,
towards his room.

That whistle set the seal on her confusion. This must
have been how her mother had felt when she had met
her father, as though she was in the grip of some
powerful, overmastering force, incapable of making any
way against it, unable to do more than keep her head
above water.

With a painful smile Mike told herself that at least
she had chosen a suitable object for her first infatuation. Guy Lórimer was handsome, he had a quick mind
and a natural authority that set him apart from other
men, and, best of all, he wasn't going to be around for
very long.

She showered quietly and went to bed. For some
minutes she lay smiling as she fantasised, then the fan-
tasies gradually became dreams.

A couple of hours later she woke and stretched with
a reminiscent smile. Almost immediately it faded. 'Oh,
hell,' she muttered, diving beneath the thin cotton sheets
to huddle there, mortified by the excesses of her un-
bridled imagination. How had he taken over her mind
and emotions so swiftly? She must, she decided with an

inward shiver as she forced herself out of bed, be horribly susceptible to male perfection.

Half an hour later she tore a strip off Sean, who confessed reluctantly that he'd forgotten to fill the outboard and promised it wouldn't happen again.

It was a difficult day. After breakfast Nola succumbed to a migraine, so for the rest of that day Mike was cook, and when she wasn't needed in the kitchen she worked in the office getting the accounts in order. Theoretically this was Harry's job, but in the mail that morning she found a couple of ominous 'account rendereds'. A quick survey of the cheque-book and the pile of accounts revealed a shambles going back at least a couple of months.

Mike shut her eyes for a horrified moment, then began to sort the piles of bills.

She had them all organised when Harry burst into the office, rumpled and disgruntled, his eyes red and his long hair hanging around his face in disarray. 'Is there a letter from England?' he asked, avoiding her dismayed eyes.

'Yes. Over there.'

Grabbing it, he ripped the envelope open and read the three sheets inside with an eagerness that had something driven in it.

Mike went back to work, trying to ignore his muttered curses.

When he'd finished he stared around the small, untidy room for some moments before asking heavily, 'How did the dance go?'

'Fine. I had to take young Simon Armstrong and Dirk What's-his-name back to Tapeka—they were drunk, and planning to sleep on the beach. I've just had a phone call from Mrs Armstrong thanking me and promising retribution.'

He nodded, but it was obvious he wasn't interested.

Mike said tentatively, 'Are you having trouble with the trustees over the lease?'

Harry stuffed the letter into his pocket. 'No. What gave you that idea? What's on tonight? Oh, it's the conservation film in the lounge, isn't it?'

'Yes. Are you going to be there?' Mike held her breath, because if he didn't turn up she was going to have to work the projector, an evil piece of equipment she was certain was possessed by a demon.

His hesitation lasted for four or five seconds. 'Yes,' he said finally, his voice weary. 'I'll be there.'

Before she had a chance to change her mind, Mike asked diffidently, 'Harry, what's the matter?'

'Nothing,' he said, walking away with the letter from the trustees sticking jauntily from his back pocket. 'Don't nag, little Mike, there's a good girl.'

'You can't go just yet,' she said quickly. 'You've got some cheques to sign.'

Without a word he came back and signed them, then left.

She didn't see Guy all that day. By the time she got to bed it was late, and she was exhausted, waking the next morning with a slight headache that probably came from sleeping too heavily.

It was a frustrating day, and the two that followed were even more so. The temperature climbed, taking, unusually for the Bay, the humidity with it. Harry appeared only occasionally, each time more morose, and completely inaccessible when a series of disasters with the plumbing culminated in a massive geyser in one of the shower blocks.

Mike rang a plumber from the mainland, who said bluntly, 'Sorry, Mike, but I'm not coming again until you've paid me for the last time.'

'It's in the mail,' she said. 'Honestly, I put it in myself yesterday.'

But he didn't come across until after the cheque arrived at midday, and when he'd fixed the leak he insisted on taking his payment with him. As she was making it out, he said, 'Mike, I want to see Harry.'

She bit her lip. 'He's not well today.'

'Then tell him that the plumbing's had it. It's going to need replacement within a couple of years, and that means megabucks.'

A hollow, aching emptiness expanded in Mike's stomach as she nodded. 'I'll tell him.'

She did when she took the cheque along to be signed. Harry was sitting in his flat, staring out of the window, and when she had told him he said indifferently, 'Yes, I know. The electricity's just about shot to pieces, too.'

'What are you going to do?'

He shrugged. 'I'll think of something.'

His attitude—the resignation and the hopelessness—frightened Mike; she had felt like this when her mother had told her she was going to die—helpless. Utterly unable in any way to affect the course of events, she had been forced to stand by and watch the inevitable happen.

That night she found it hard to sleep, so it was with shadows under her eyes that she spent the morning cleaning out cabins before going in to Paihia to pick up eight more guests. She picked at her lunch, then went through the menu for the following month with Nola. When that was done she put her head down on her arms, sighing, 'Lord, it's hot.'

Nola said firmly, 'And you're tired; you've got great dark circles under your eyes. You've done more than enough for today; why don't you go for a swim? Everyone else will be resting.'

'Most of them are out today anyway, on cruises or diving.' Mike stood up. Now that she had stopped an unfamiliar restlessness gripped her. The thought of soaking away her aches and inchoate fears in cool, buoyant water was enormously appealing. It might even get rid of her headache.

'I'll walk over to Tuesday Bay,' she said, giving a decisive little nod.

'How's that man doing?' Nola asked casually. 'The
handsome one who arrived four or five days ago? You
know, the one you danced with.'

Sean looked up from the sink where he was getting
himself a glass of water. 'The Lorimer guy? He's doing
everything,' he said, relieving a somewhat flushed Mike
from the necessity of answering. 'It's funny, though. He
doesn't seem to be on holiday. He asks too many questions. That is, when he can flick off the women.' He
leered lasciviously. 'Wish I had a tenth of his pull.'

Nola, who was his wife, eyed him with a tolerant smile
and said, 'What do you mean, he's not on holiday? Why
would he be here if he wasn't on holiday?'

Sean shrugged. 'Oh, I don't know,' he said vaguely.
'He looks at things too hard, if you get me.'

'He's that sort,' Nola said. 'You can tell. Interested
in everything.'

Mike escaped. She had only seen glimpses of Guy these
last few days, almost always accompanied by an adoring
coterie of women. Not, she had noted, that he seemed
to flirt overtly like some men, all teeth and unsubtle
glances, with shirts unbuttoned and skin-tight shorts.
Guy didn't need such blatant preening; his vivid maleness
ensured that he attracted attention without trying for it.

Shame at her susceptibility ensured that even if Mike
hadn't been so busy she'd have done her best to keep
her distance.

Banishing him firmly from her mind, she went back
home and got ready for a swim. The protection afforded
by olive skin wouldn't save her from the fierce northern
sun for more than twenty minutes, so she donned a shirt
that covered her arms, royal blue shorts, a pair of sand-
shoes and an old sunhat with a floppy brim. In a bag
with her towel was water-repellent sun-screen, a bottle
of orange juice, and a hard-hitting novel she'd been
trying to read for the last three months.

Luckily, she didn't droop in the heat. It was lack of
sleep that gave her the niggling headache—if Mike didn't

have eight hours' sleep she woke with an uncertain temper and a thick head.

Her legs carried her easily up the short but steep track that led from the hotel to Tuesday Beach. The sun dazzled down, wilting the short grass, summoning balsam from the manuka scrub, so that she walked along in a piquant, minty, hazy atmosphere. Tiny blue and brown moths fluttered over the grass, as silent as the cicadas were noisy.

Mike's headache began to ease; she was smiling when she breasted the ridge. The view there always had the power to stop her heart with its sheer beauty. In front stretched an expanse of water coloured an intense turquoise that sang of summer. Contrasting with it were the tawny islands, variegated by an occasional dark blue one which had bush on it. White-winged yachts swayed noiselessly by, and the bay was scattered with small dinghies where dedicated fishers sat waiting for their prey.

As she always did, she went across to the small plot where Harry's wife, Dodo, had demanded her ashes be buried overlooking the view she had loved so well. Putting the lilac and white heads of agapanthus in the jar, Mike said aloud, 'It's a beautiful day.'

Below her, the white sand of Tuesday Beach curved invitingly, bare of people. Pleased, Mike ran down the steep little slope. She had had enough of people today! Within five minutes she had stripped off in the convenient shade of one of the immense pohutukawa trees to reveal a pared-down violet *maillot*, an expensive buy she had succumbed to the year before. After stashing her clothes behind a root she anointed herself with sunblock, then raced across the sizzling sand so quickly that it barely had time to burn the tender soles of her feet.

The water was blissfully cool, soon soothing away the last remnants of her headache. A good swimmer, made excellent by the long hours she spent in the water, she arrowed out to sea for quite some time before turning over to rest.

Her hands made little flirting motions in the water as she looked up into a sky so burning, so vibrant a blue, that she had to narrow her eyes against its glare. Rainbows formed and coalesced on her lashes.

Mike sighed. She loved summer, revelled in the hot days and warm nights, adored the Bay in holiday guise. Other seasons had their own particular charms, but summer was when the Bay came into its own.

The throb of engines had impinged for some minutes before she realised that the boat was actually heading towards her. If they weren't keeping a good look-out she could be in some danger. Sometimes holiday-makers were inexcusably careless.

A quick swivel in the water revealed that it was the hotel runabout, and it was coming towards her. Perhaps, she thought with a grin, someone had seen her out and raised the alarm. It certainly wasn't someone who worked at Far Winds; they all knew she could swim like a fish.

Amusement turned to an odd mixture of delight and dismay when she recognised the man at the wheel. Just her luck, she thought hollowly, for it to be Guy Lorimer. Damn! She had tried so hard to put him from her mind, and almost succeeded. She certainly didn't want to see him now.

Fate, in its usual unjust way, had decided otherwise.

The engines throttled back, and he leaned over the side, his questioning blue gaze fixed on to her face. 'Are you all right?'

Close up the cleanly etched, unqualified beauty of his features was breathtaking. 'Yes, I'm fine.' Treading water, Mike pushed her hair back from her face, feeling that intent survey right down to her toes. 'Thank you,' she added politely.

'You'd better get in and I'll take you back to shore. You must be a mile out.'

Firmly Mike shook her head. 'No, it's all right; I'm quite capable of swimming back.'

'I'm sure you are.' Guy smiled, but she saw that stubborn purpose in both the smile and his regard. 'However, I'll feel happier if I make sure you get there.'

Her pale gaze sharpened. 'That's ridiculous! I've been swimming off here all my life. I'm in no danger——'

'Nevertheless,' he interrupted, completely unruffled, 'I'll stay with you until you get there.' He waited for a moment, but when she made no attempt to do anything other than stare at him his tone sharpened. 'Give me your hands and I'll haul you in.'

Antagonism flared to life in Mike, tightening the wide softness of her mouth, honing her eyes into narrowed points of brilliance.

The smile he gave her was hard-edged and challenging, but it highlighted a sudden smouldering charm that made Mike's heart stop in her throat.

'All right,' he said softly, 'I believe you. You can swim like a mermaid; you can make it back without the slightest puff. I suppose you developed long-distance swimming to get away from people like me.'

Mike grinned. He laughed down at her, and she sank beneath the water to escape that teasing regard.

When she emerged, blowing bubbles, he said, 'I want to look at the reef. Would you like to come?'

Put like that, of course, she didn't want to say no. Mike cast her common sense into the depths. He wasn't going to be here for much longer, so she was quite safe. But her hands shook as she extended them in mute surrender.

Without exerting much effort, Guy drew her smoothly out of the water and on to the deck. Water streamed down her in a transparent glittering cloak that hid nothing of sleek, strong limbs and feminine curves. Mike felt altogether too exposed in her sexy violet swimming-suit.

Guy eyed her with a frank appreciation that somehow robbed his survey of impertinence. 'You gave me quite a jolt when I saw you in the water. I'm not accustomed to coming across anyone swimming so far off shore. Fossick around in that chilly-bin and get yourself a drink.'

'All right,' she said, fossicking. 'I am thirsty. But we'll have to go in to the beach to pick up my clothes before we take off for the reef. I don't want to get sunburnt.'

'Fair enough.' Sensibly, he had pulled a T-shirt on over his swimming-trunks.

Telling herself sternly that she wasn't going to act like a stupid, easily impressed little idiot, Mike got herself a can of soft drink, and a beer for him.

From somewhere she managed to dredge up enough composure to say something as she looked into a face that managed to stay unreadable even when he was smiling with that frightening charm, as potent and as dangerous as a fallen angel. Only too clearly, nothing significant was happening to him.

For some reason she wanted him, desperately, with an ardour that had nothing to do with common sense or reason or logic, a desire that was primitive and fierce, untamed by any constraints, existing of itself and for itself.

Mike recognised the dark undertone to her wild response. It was solely physical, the pull of potent, addictive male for nubile female, physical attraction that was more potent than champagne, but ultimately as ephemeral.

The primal mating urge was no respecter of persons. Although Guy Lorimer looked as though he could offer sexual delights in full, such imperiously masculine creatures were usually conceited and arrogant and demanding.

Watch it, she told herself bleakly. She knew what happened to women who gave in to mindless passion; she was the result of such an encounter. She had no intention of repeating her mother's mistake.

But when Guy raised the beer can and drank the contents, she watched the muscles move in the strong brown column of his throat and shivered.

'You're cold,' he said instantly, smoky steel-blue eyes never leaving her face. 'Here, put this around you.' He reached down and picked up a towelling wrap, tossing it across to her.

'Thanks.' Yanking the wrap close, she tied the belt with jerky, defiant movements.

His lashes drooped. 'Hide as much of your body as you can,' he said evenly, 'but you've still got the fatal magic of a mermaid: black hair with the devil's crimson lurking in each wave; pale, magical eyes; sleek, tantalising limbs and skin as warm and bloomy as a peach. Mermaids are dangerous, but any sailor would scoop you up from the sea.'

Blushing furiously, as much with anger at her own lack of sophistication as at his words, Mike said curtly, 'You don't need to make fun of me.'

His mouth was still curled in a faint, hard smile, but he said with a surprising gentleness, 'I'm not making fun of you, Mike. You're a delectable little thing, but I keep forgetting how young you are.'

'Twenty isn't that much younger than twenty-six.'

'It's not so much the years as the experience,' he said, and the smile became cynical, almost without humour. 'Right, let's get those clothes.'

He turned the wheel. Unable to think of anything else to do, Mike sipped the cool soft drink gratefully, easing its refreshing tartness down her dry throat while his words buzzed through her brain, tantalising, exciting...

She had been a fool to come on board. She should have turned and swum back to shore, and not let that stupid streak of recklessness surface. It always got her into trouble.

But when they were only a few yards off the beach he said, 'Are you in a hurry? I haven't been to this beach before and I'd like to have a look at it.'

'I don't have to be back until five,' she said, surrendering.

'Great.'

His idea of seeing a beach was to walk along it and scramble up the ridge behind, and sit looking out over the island and the sea. Sean was right; Guy wanted to know everything. Mike pointed out various islands and places on the mainland, told him their history, how high the hills were, who owned each farm and island and holiday cottage, and some of the more repeatable tales. She had never had an audience so interested in her domain.

CHAPTER THREE

As THE runabout idled through the glittering water on the way to the reef, Mike noticed that Guy knew exactly what he was doing with it. Which made the fact that he was prepared to let her take the wheel more surprising. Many men couldn't believe that a woman could actually steer a boat as well as a man, even when the woman was experienced and the man was not. She had become an expert in body language, the tiny betraying signals that indicated just how uneasy some men could get when they considered a woman to be operating outside her area of expertise. Chauvinism was alive and unrepentant in New Zealand.

Clearly Guy Lorimer's confidence was bone-deep. He had nothing to prove, no deep-seated insecurity that forced him to try to prove his masculine superiority over and over again.

'Harry was going to organise a petition to have this reef made into a marine reserve,' she said as they skirted a rusty outcrop. 'The fish have always clustered round it, so it would be the perfect place. The locals leave it alone because most of them believe it acts as a seed bed for the rest of the Bay, and not many visiting fishermen know it's here, so it's not fished out.'

'What happened? Why didn't he go ahead with it?'

She looked away from those too perceptive eyes. 'Oh, he never really got the time,' she said vaguely. Over the years Harry had had plenty of good ideas, but somehow he lacked the staying power to carry them through. Which was why, she thought with a mental grimace, although Harry and the district power board had discussed getting electricity to Far Winds through a marine cable, they were still coping with a temperamental generator. Good idea, just never acted on.

Guy seemed to have lost interest in the vagaries of Harry's mind. Leaning over the side, he said, 'I brought a snorkel with me. Let's take turns.'

As always the reef was aflutter with fish, not the glowing, neon inhabitants of tropical reefs, but still beautiful, and remarkably tame. Eager to reveal its glories, determined that he should appreciate it, Mike showed Guy the most densely populated areas, and when he came up for the second time asked, 'What do you think?'

'It's glorious.' With the easy grace and power of a sea creature, he climbed aboard.

The westering sun poured over him in a flood of golden light, catching every drop of water, so that for an instant he seemed like some unique pagan statue carved of crystals. Each smooth, fluid curve of muscle, each long line of sinew and bone, each angular feature glittered in a radiance that stabbed Mike straight to the heart.

Something of her bemused reaction must have shown in her face. His eyes darkened; for a long, deliberate moment they stared at each other, then his gaze dropped and lingered on the soft contours of her body, sleek and compact in the skin-tight violet *maillot*. Captured by that unwavering, heated survey, the breath stopped in Mike's throat. A pang of sensation, quick and passionate, lanced her body. She licked the salt from lips that were suddenly tingling and hot.

Guy said harshly, 'Do you know what you're doing?' but kissed the answer from her mouth, his own wet and cool yet oddly warm.

For all the protection the material of her swimsuit gave her, they might as well have been naked. The shudder that flicked across Mike's skin like a cold breeze on a hot day disappeared, replaced by incandescent heat where their slick bodies touched and caught fire. His fierce, famished mouth summoned a like wildness from her.

She made a noise deep in her throat, a kind of gasping sigh, and wound her arms around his neck, offering herself to him in a movement that was innocently explicit.

Immediately he let her go, all expression disappearing from his features as he reimposed control. Mike's knees sagged; she collapsed on to the seat, shame and bewilderment chasing each other through her eyes.

The grimness left his face. He said unhurriedly, 'Not at all fishy, which I imagine a mermaid must be. Here, dry yourself. You're shivering.'

She was shivering because those seconds in his arms had shown her why people made such a fuss about sex. For just a moment he had felt it too, that primitive fever in the blood.

And now she was cold as she had never been before.

'I'd better get back,' she said abruptly, hiding her face in the towel, turning away under the pretext of drying her shoulders and arms. 'I have to be on Reception at five. A group of people are arriving. From Germany, mostly, I think.' She was babbling, trying to hide with the sound of her voice the slow smoulder of sensation that burned deep in her body.

'OK, we'll head straight back.' He switched on the engine, guiding the little boat around the jagged rocks of the reef before heading for the wharf. 'You work too hard,' he said. 'Whenever I've seen you these last few days you've been scurrying around like a harried possum.'

Lifting a negligent shoulder, she returned casually, 'I'm used to it.'

'You shouldn't be,' he said sharply. He stopped there, but his disapproval was plain.

His concern bathed Mike in a warm, secure feeling, until she recognised the danger and rejected it. In a way, such weakness was even more debilitating than her helpless response to his masculinity.

Deliberately, she kept her eyes averted from his sleek, darkly bronzed body. She had seen hundreds of men dressed in as little, yet until Guy had exploded into her life not one had ever set primeval tides surging through her. If she closed her eyes she could see him imprinted on her brain, the long, powerful arms and legs, the way the muscles flexed and relaxed whenever he moved, the fine black hair on his chest scrolling across skin as gleaming and silky as a seal's before arrowing into a suggestive point at the waistband of the indigo racing briefs he wore.

Determinedly she turned her face away, until a hint from untold generations of female ancestors made her wonder whether she was being too obvious, whether her reserve would make him realise how strongly affected she was by him.

She sneaked a sideways look, only to meet his blue eyes, cool, unreadable, deliberately guarded. Embarrassment whipped colour into her cheeks. Determinedly pinning a smile to her mouth, she began to point out every cove and headland, every terraced pa site, every pohutukawa tree.

He asked more questions, and soon she found herself telling him of the ambivalence of the locals about tourism, their appreciation that the local economy was founded on it yet their dislike of the disadvantages—the sometimes crass commercialism of the buildings and concepts, the noise and crowds over the summer period, and some holiday-makers' offhand attitude to the Bay the locals loved so well.

'We need a longer season,' she said at last, as Far Winds came into view. 'Winter can be very pleasant up here, not too wet and not too cold, and autumn is usually lovely. But nobody's trying hard for tourists then; everyone seems content to cream the summer crop.'

'You've thought of this quite seriously, haven't you?'

He wasn't being patronising, but she bristled nevertheless; only good manners stopped her from a sharp rejoinder. 'Everyone talks and thinks about it,' she said a little remotely. 'It's vitally important to us.'

'Most girls of your age seem more interested in clothes and boyfriends than the ecology of a tourist area.'

'You must move in restricted circles,' she said crisply.

He grinned down at her, bold and brash and confident as a pirate. 'It seems as though I must,' he said solemnly, then turned his full attention to easing in the runabout.

He didn't seem in any hurry to leave the wharf; for long seconds he stood looking at the long peninsula of scrub-covered land that backed the beach and the tree-covered hillsides beyond with distant, measuring eyes.

A shudder worked its way down Mike's spine. At that moment he reminded her of a Viking with a fresh country in his sights, ripe for plunder. The austere line of his jaw emphasised an unfaltering strength she found very intimidating.

Then he looked at her, laughter glinting in his eyes, and that faint premonition faded. 'Just about paradise,' he said, urging her forward with a hand at her waist. 'You've got twenty minutes before you have to be at Reception. Is there any entertainment tonight?'

'A walk to hear the kiwis at ten o'clock. Thank you for a super afternoon.'

He said roughly, 'You're very sweet,' and bent his head and kissed her.

His mouth was warm and seeking, oddly tender. Mike didn't even think of resisting. She kissed him back, her body melting into his.

She had heard people say the world stood still, and had accepted it as a transparent cliché, a pardonable exaggeration to describe the indescribable. But for one transcendent moment the world seemed to wait, motionless, while she lost herself in this man's kiss.

It affected him, too. She felt him take a deep breath, heard him mutter something that sounded like a curse before he kissed her again, and this time there was no holding back. His tongue touched the soft line of her lips; it was Mike's turn to stiffen, but with artless, hungry curiosity she opened her mouth for him. He explored the soft depths yielded to him with a passion that was fire and wine, like sweet, warm rain after a long, hard drought, like nothing she had ever experienced in her life before.

Dimly she was aware that people on the beach could see them, but she couldn't resist the enchantment of his kiss. Strange heated tides coursed through her bloodstream, tides as fierce and inevitable as a lava flow.

At last Guy lifted his head and stared down at her with dazed, smoky eyes. Mike took an alarmed step backwards, scanning his face with a gaze that had gone from slumbrous to horrified almost instantaneously.

'I have to go,' she gabbled, and shot up the salty wooden steps to the wharf, not looking behind her.

That one last look had seared his face on to her brain. He had stared at her as though she was something he had hoped never to see again; in spite of their dense, exotic colouring his eyes had been cold, almost opaque, and there had been no smile on the wide, sensual mouth.

Mike never remembered getting to the cottage, any more than she remembered dragging the gate open, or walking up the path, or opening her front door.

Once inside she sank down into a chair and covered her burning ears and cheeks with her hands. She must have been mad, kissing him like that in full view of everybody on the beach! Although common sense told her that there was always an observer, always someone who watched, she could only hope that everybody had been too busy with their own affairs to notice.

Getting up heavily, she made her way to the shabby bathroom.

In spite of the hurly-burly of Reception, she found it difficult to concentrate; Guy's kisses had thrown her into such turmoil that she had to force herself to keep her mind on what she was doing.

She wished fervently that he would go so that she could resume her life without these violent swings in her emotions. Once he was out of the way she'd eventually forget him, or recall him with nothing more than amused fondness.

There had been other kisses, of course, quite frequent ones, but the fumbling embraces of boys her age hadn't affected her at all. Her mother had been strict, so there hadn't been opportunities for anything more than kisses. Mike didn't know when she had first realised that her parents were unmarried, but she had grown up knowing that her mother feared physical desire and was afraid that Mike too might fall victim to its powerful lures. Popular at school, Mike could have made time for experimentation, but she had loved her mother too much to go against her wishes.

And for the last four years she simply hadn't had the time or the energy or the inclination to do anything more than lightly flirt with those men who had made it obvious they found her attractive.

Which left her, she thought as she tossed and turned in her bed that night, oddly naïve. That must be why Guy's kisses had rocketed her so far off balance. She had thought herself reasonably worldly, even if much of her attitude had been gained second-hand; it was a shock to realise that, although she didn't regret missing the flirtations and affairs other girls of her age indulged in, she was so incredibly vulnerable to a man's untamed sensuality.

But of course Guy was not just any man. He was special and important to her in a way no other man had ever been.

He had been surprised, too. Her eyes glittered like pale jewels and one hand clenched between her breasts as she remembered the dark hunger in his glance, the sudden harsh indrawn breath that had lifted his chest, the way his whole body had tensed.

Yes, she thought soberly, trying to put the whole episode in its correct place; he had wanted her for that moment just as much as she had wanted him. And, firmly squelching the unbidden spark of excitement that thought engendered, she reminded herself of her father, who had wanted her mother, coaxed her into falling in love with him, and then left her, pregnant and so shattered by his betrayal that she had never been able to love another man.

Men see these things differently, her mother had told her when an adolescent Mike had asked her about it. She had said little about the man who had seduced and betrayed her, but Mike knew what he looked like, for she bore her heritage in her face. The curly black hair, the wide cheekbones and squared-off chin came from her father, not her pretty, delicately featured mother.

Her hand drifted up to her mouth. It was slightly tender, and for a moment she thought she could taste Guy on her lips. 'Don't be an idiot,' she told herself brusquely as she kicked off the sheet.

Love, sex, desire, whatever the terminology, was dangerous for a woman in ways that didn't apply to a man. It made women vulnerable, uncontrolled, stripped away their ability to think and behave logically, to function properly.

Guy might be attracted to her, but she knew perfectly well that he wasn't in the least interested in her as a person. How could he be? He didn't know anything about her and they had nothing in common. He was rich, and more than a little spoiled, a man whose polished sophistication was inborn in him.

Firmly setting her mouth, Mike tried to banish him from her mind. It was useless fretting and worrying. He was just a guest, one who'd soon be gone.

And if in some hidden region of her heart she hoped, the fleeting glimpse she'd had of him as she'd gone back through the hotel after her shift put paid to any further foolishness. He'd been walking towards the beach with a woman. Neither of them had seen her; they had been far too absorbed in each other.

Just recalling it brought back the jealousy that had torn through Mike. The colour seeped from her skin, leaving her sallow and sharp-featured. Each breath was like a lance to her heart. This had to stop, and stop now. It hurt too much.

Finally she got to sleep, but her rest was disturbed by dreams, and she awoke well before dawn the next morning, dark snatches of those dreams chasing themselves around her tired brain.

Just what was it that so impressed her about the wretched man? Not merely his looks, although they satisfied her human hunger for beauty and symmetry. Not his build, although he had the lean, functional elegance of an athlete, a stripped grace that stirred her unbearably. Somehow he transcended his physical attributes.

Nor was it the careless arrogance of wealth and social position. In fact, that grated on her. Not, she thought shrewdly, that he was a snob; he just hadn't ever known what it was like to worry about money, or background, or what people would say about him.

He had an authority she had never seen before, a deep inner assurance. When he walked into a room people looked at him. It was as simple as that. His power was an essential part of him; it didn't come from his money or his background or his social position. Set him down on the traditional desert island, bereft of everything but his brain and his body, and he would still be powerful, still manage to dominate his environment.

The pictures this brought to mind were too alluring. For a few minutes Mike drifted in the warm seas of fantasy, only to be rudely jerked into the everyday world by the telephone's shrill summons.

'Can you act as a tour guide today?' the receptionist asked anxiously. 'Everyone else is busy, and a client wants to do a quick tour of all the islands. Harry says you're to go.'

Hastily Mike checked her agenda. What she'd planned to do that day could wait until tomorrow, so she said, 'Yes, all right. When do we start?'

'He'll be down at the wharf at eight. Sean'll have the boat gassed up and ready to go, and Nola's packing a hamper right now.'

'OK.' Mike yawned, and hung up. Half an hour later she was just about to leave when the phone bleeped once more. This time it was Harry.

'Did you get that letter posted to England?' he asked.

'Yes, it went out on the mail yesterday.' It was not like Harry to fuss.

'OK, love. I'll see you later.'

Black brows lifted in surprise, she picked up her bag and went through the door. It was cool but there was no wind, and the sky, radiantly clear as a great glass bell, held the promise of a magnificent day.

At the wharf the small day cruiser rocked gently in the wake of a launch that was chugging earnestly down the passage. Mike strode lightly down the steps to the pontoon.

Out into the cockpit, tall and lithe and wide-shouldered, came Guy. Assailed once more by that terrifying feeling of primal recognition, Mike's insides liquefied. What's happening to me? she wondered despairingly.

Calm down, her sturdy common sense demanded. There was no soul calling to soul about this; it was simply a violent physical attraction. It wasn't even something she could do anything about, as her body seemed to acknowledge no restraints.

'Good morning, Mike.' He sounded urbane, a little amused, but she registered a hint of some darker emotion in his tone.

'You want to go around the islands, I gather.' Her voice was stiff, but not obviously so.

'Yes. All the privately owned ones.'

Her brows rose as she swung into the boat, but although he acknowledged her curiosity with a hard little smile he didn't satisfy it. Ah, well, on Far Winds the guest was king.

And that was how she had to think of him; he was a guest, nothing more.

But as they moved slowly away from the wharf Mike glanced over her shoulder. Some strange atavistic instinct told her that today was some sort of turning-point in her life; if she went out with Guy she was not going to come home the same person. There would be no going back; events would be set in motion which were going to affect her in ways as yet unknown.

Superstitious nonsense, her practical mind scoffed, but she was racked by an uneasiness not diminished by the fact that it was without foundation.

She tried to suppress it. She had always loved the sea, loved showing people the Bay, and this was just another day spent doing that. However, when they headed down Albert Passage Guy came to stand beside her, and her apprehension returned in full measure.

'Where do you want to go first?' she asked, striving for a businesslike intonation.

'Oh, I put myself into your hands,' he said drily. His burnished gaze came to rest on Mike's averted profile.

The touch of insolence in his tone dragged her eyes around to his face. His smile was slow and lazy, and once more she suffered that disconcerting lurch in the pit of her stomach.

'Do you want to go the tourist route?' she asked shortly, using briskness to mask the defiant note in her words. 'Out to the Cape, through the hole in the rock and back? Because if you do, it would have been a lot cheaper to go on one of the scheduled trips.'

The strident sound of one of the tourist vessels' sirens came as a welcome interruption to the jumble of reactions and emotions that passed for thoughts in her brain at that moment. She waved, and the people hanging over the side waved back; she smiled half-heartedly at the cameras pointing in their direction.

'No,' Guy said calmly, 'I don't want to do that. Don't you like having your photo taken?'

'No.'

'Why not?'

She shrugged. 'I feel like a caged monkey.'

'Not a monkey,' he said. He allowed his eyes to rove the contours of her face with speculative appreciation.

That was how it started, but it soon developed into something Mike was not prepared to deal with. Her mouth compressed into a thin line.

'No, not a monkey,' he said after several prickly moments. 'Something small and pretty and sleek and self-possessed. A kitten, probably.'

He wasn't flirting with her; there was something too deliberate and purposeful in his survey.

Her mind raced furiously. 'Thanks,' she said, keeping her voice cool and uninvolved. 'I think.'

'Don't you like being called a kitten?'

'Would you like being called a pup?'

His eyes narrowed into slits of pure colour, so brilliant that all emotions were burned out by the concentrated fire. Mike had to stop herself from turning tail, because those shafts of light pierced right into her soul. Then he smiled, and the potent masculine charm washed over her with all the force and inevitability of a breaking wave.

'No,' he said urbanely. 'There's something intrinsically plebeian about a pup.'

'And something intrinsically helpless about a kitten,' she retorted. 'I'm not helpless.'

He grinned. 'Far from it. All right, I won't call you a kitten. I prefer mermaid, anyway. Unlike kittens, mermaids are inherently dangerous.'

This reference to yesterday rendered Mike even more uneasy, but she struggled to make her voice light and impersonal, as though he was just another tourist to be shown the beauties of the Bay.

'Where do you want to go first?' she asked.

He looked ahead. 'Those are islands we're looking at, aren't they?'

'Yes. You can't see them all from here; they lie one behind another. But Moturua is the closest one, and then there's Motukiekie, and Urupukapuka, which is the biggest. You can just see Waewaetorea, and the one to the north is Okahu, commonly known as Red Head because it's got a huge red cliff on it. They're all lovely, but I like Far Winds best.'

'Why?'

She shrugged. 'There's a hint of mystery, of otherworldliness, about it.'

Half expecting him to tease, she braced herself. But he mused, 'Atmosphere is an interesting quality. Some places that are breathtakingly beautiful don't have it. It's like charm. Physical attributes have nothing to do with it. I wonder why?'

Staring ahead, Mike said, 'I don't know about human beings, but I think to have atmosphere places must appeal to the imagination. Far Winds is beautiful and peaceful, with everything an island should have—hills and trees and exquisite beaches, lovely lagoons. There was a shipwreck on it once, and Captain Cook visited it when he was exploring the Pacific, and there's even a legend about a very beautiful Maori woman who ran away with her lover and lived happily there.' She stopped, afraid she was revealing too much.

'So you like danger and mystery and romance,' he commented, watching her through long lashes.

'Only when they're safely in the past,' she retorted promptly.

His teeth gleamed white as he grinned, something reckless showing for a second in his expression. He turned his head and said, 'Really? Ah, that must be

Tuesday Bay, mustn't it, where I picked you up yesterday.'

His choice of words was careless, to say the least. Mike refused to rise to the bait, if bait it was. 'Yes,' she said calmly.

'How far out were you planning to swim?'

She shrugged again, shoulders moving too abruptly beneath the gold material of her cotton shirt. 'I'd got as far as I'd intended,' she said, her voice flat and unstressed.

'Is that your normal distance, or did you make an extra effort that day?'

Did he think she had swum out deliberately to attract his attention? Fuming, she looked up sharply, but he was gazing across the wide, dazzlingly green waters of the Bay, out past the entrance to the stormy Pacific Ocean that didn't stop until it bumped up against South America.

Mike caught a flick of movement from the corner of her eye. 'Dolphins,' she exclaimed on a note of joy. 'Oh, look, there they are!'

Immediately they were all about the cruiser, sleek, streamlined things with their mouths curled in a perpetual smile, leaping and frolicking in the bow wave with every appearance of transparent delight.

'It's Old Neptune and his family,' Mike said, eyes sparkling in her glowing, excited face as she cut the engine back.

'How do you know?'

'Well, they're common dolphins; you can tell from the figure-of-eight markings on their flanks, and because they're so enthusiastic. Bottle-nosed dolphins are silver-grey, and they're much more sedate. And then the big male—see, that one—he's got a scar down his side. This family is our resident one.'

'Do you see them often?'

She smiled. 'Yes. Oh, look, there's a new baby. What a darling little thing!'

At that moment the peaked cap on her head was flipped off by a vagrant gust. A quick lunge rescued it, but she overstretched and slipped. Instantly she was seized by two iron hands.

'Be careful!' Guy's voice was harsh.

It took her brain a second or two to catch up, but when it did she realised she was standing with her face pressed into his shoulder, imprisoned against the tense rigidity of a body held in complete, involuntary stasis.

Mike couldn't breathe, yet she drowned in his scent, slightly salty, powerfully masculine. It slid past all the defences her mind had built, straight through by the back door into the most vulnerable part of her, her sensuality. Without volition her tongue came out and, delicately cat-like, she licked the bronzed throat where his pulse thudded heavily. His taste flooded her mouth, her being, rousing hungers like flimsily chained beasts inside her.

For a long, frozen moment his muscles stayed locked. Then he stepped back, almost pushing her away from him with ungentle hands. Appalled by her temerity, Mike stared up into a face that was drawn and savage with fiercely suppressed emotion.

'That was probably not a good idea,' he said through barely moving lips.

She touched her dry inner mouth with her tongue. 'I didn't mean to——'

'You didn't mean to be as provocative as you possibly could? You didn't want to put your mark on me?' Something feral prowled in his voice, in his eyes. 'That's hard to believe, Mike. Don't let your tendency to flirt run away with you. Teases often get more than they bargain for.'

He turned her around so that she could once more look out at Old Neptune and his extended family, his arm like a steel bar across her shoulders.

Mike had the unnerving feeling that she had been cut out, separated from the rest of humanity, and that until he was ready to release her that was where she'd stay. If he had wanted to intimidate her, he was succeeding.

'I am not a tease,' she said angrily.

'No? A flirt, then.'

'Not that either.'

With a movement that was almost vicious she revved up the engine, sending the little craft surging through the water. Instantly the dolphins altered speed to stay in their favourite spot, on the crest of the waves forced out on either side by the bow.

'You have a way of looking up through your lashes that is very hard to resist. I doubt if you even know you're doing it,' he said austerely, 'but that was a fairly fervent kiss I saw you exchange with the band leader the other night. Is he your boyfriend?'

'No, he is not. He was just being silly.'

'I see.' His voice was dry.

Mike kept her gaze fixed ahead, so conscious of her wildfire physical reaction to his closeness that she took in nothing of the exhilarating scene in front. Through her heavy lashes the water glinted, silver and blue-green, the dolphins' lustrous bodies curving through the foam in a celebration of grace and delight.

Normally she would have revelled in the moment, embraced it with all the spirited enthusiasm of her nature. Now she was buffeted by an alien need, a merciless summons entirely different from the sparkling beauty of the day, yet part of it too. Guy's arm was heavy, commanding, as though he was trying to impress her with some message. If he was, she thought with a mixture of anger and despair, he was failing. The only message she got came from her body.

'Look!' she exclaimed, pointing.

The big male, sleek and glorious in his pride, suddenly hurtled out of the water and hung tail-down, suspended, it seemed, for long seconds above the surface, before falling in with a monstrous splash.

'Showing off.' Guy's voice was amused, as though she had never touched him and he had never threatened her.

She tried to match it. 'Or perhaps it's just the sheer joy of being alive.'

'Perhaps. But I imagine the presence of several impressionable females has something to do with it. Look, he's doing it again.'

Mike waited until the dolphins had sped away to port before asking with delicate scorn, 'Do all men like to show off?'

'Yes.' His darkly textured voice was wry, a little cynical. 'It's part of nature. Males strut their stuff and females pick the one who catches their eye. Why should the human race be any different?'

Trying to imagine him 'strutting his stuff,' Mike failed lamentably. He didn't need to indulge in such overt displays of power and virility. Self-possession, allied to his vital physical beauty, meant that boasting, however subtle, would be superfluous and counter-productive. Besides, she suspected that an innate pride forbade it.

'Why indeed?' she asked a little acidly. 'But are we just animals? What about love?'

'Love?'

Mike reacted to the taunt in his voice with a spurt of anger. She didn't know much about love between men and women, but she had seen enough instances of it in her lifetime to convince her that it happened to some lucky people. 'It exists.'

Irony robbed his smile of humour. 'Most women use love as a bargaining counter in their search for security of some sort.'

'*Bargaining counter*?' Suddenly furious, she sent him a haughty look. 'What an arrogant, sexist thing to say!'

A cynical little smile twisted his mouth. 'It's the truth. Marriage is the bartering of sexual and social advantages for security,' he said contemplatively, watching her from half-closed eyes.

'If that's the way you think,' she said, shrugging, 'it's no wonder you're not married. No woman would have you.'

His brows winged up, whether in surprise or distaste at her frankness was difficult to tell. Mike stared back at him doggedly, refusing to back down.

'How do you know I'm not married?'

Of course she didn't know. Plenty of men were married before they reached twenty-six. 'Are you?' she asked, trying to sound as though it didn't matter a bit to her one way or the other.

He shook his black head. 'No.'

There was a note of finality to the word that grated across nerves already abraded by his touch, his presence.

Mike said slowly, 'Well, there you are, then.' A frown pleated her dark brows. 'Perhaps security *is* part of the bargain, but women need reassurance, some sort of commitment, so they have help when it comes to bringing up children.'

It had been a struggle for her mother; she could remember days when Linda had frowned and snapped, and as Mike had grown older she had come to realise just how difficult it had been for her mother to care for her, not just financially, but emotionally. If Linda hadn't had to struggle alone, her life would have been a lot easier.

'I know. Which simply means that the desire for security is programmed into feminine genes.' Guy gave her a mocking smile. 'I don't blame your gender for it; I accept it. But it's hypocritical to admit that I'm right then call me a cynic for saying so.'

He had her nicely. She stared at him in frustration until her mouth quirked. 'So why do *men* marry,' she asked sweetly, 'if it's not for security?'

He shrugged. 'Of course it's for security. Most men want children they know are their own.'

'It's a wise child that knows its own father.' Her voice was sardonic. She knew her father's name, nothing more. It was all she wanted to know.

'My children,' Guy said, his voice level, 'will definitely know their own father.' In spite of the lack of expression in both his voice and his face a dark, implacable intensity burned below the surface.

'This is Waewaetorea,' Mike said, unable to respond in any other way.

'Who owns it?'

She told him and cut the engine simultaneously. The cruiser settled back into the water to move sedately towards a sweep of silver-white beach. In the still water between the headlands their wake was a feather of foam, straight and delicately traced behind them.

'We're here,' Mike said inanely, promising herself that she wasn't going to get involved in any more disturbing conversations with Guy. From now on she would stick to social platitudes. 'Would you like to look around by yourself?'

'No. You can show it to me.'

That day they visited all the privately owned islands, landing on some, circling others. Guy asked her questions about them all, the questions becoming more penetrating as he realised just how wide her knowledge was. He seemed fascinated by what she had to tell him, and she became drunk on appreciation and the sun, drunk on his presence.

At about three o'clock he said, 'Let's go back to Far Winds. I haven't had a good look at all three lagoons. Can we come in from the other side?'

'Yes, of course.'

Half an hour later they were walking along the beach of one of the exquisite little lagoons, its almost circular sheet of shallow water guarded from the full force of the easterlies by low pohutukawa-clad headlands and hills.

'I love this place,' Mike said on a sigh. 'It's so beautiful!'

'It is indeed.' He looked about keenly. 'Who owns it?'

'A family trust in England somewhere.'

Throughout the rest of the lazy afternoon, while they swam in the warm, translucent waters of the lagoons and she showed him some of the intriguing creatures that lived there, explored the tree-clad headlands and bluffs, then ate the left-overs from lunch on the white sand beneath the massive swooping branches of a pohutukawa tree, Mike felt a strange, fretful tension grow within her, made the more palpable by the placid beauty of their surroundings.

It was just self-consciousness, of course. Try as she did, she couldn't rid her mind—or her body—of the memory of those kisses yesterday.

Which was stupid, because, if one thing was certain, it was that Guy had put them completely from his mind. Probably they hadn't meant much to him, anyway. She had inflated a few sunny moments to something important in her life, whereas to him they would be nothing but a flirtation. Humiliation crawled beneath her skin, stronger because she had to hide it. She couldn't dismiss it, but she could at least strive to be his equal in sophistication, in composure.

When the tea flask had been drained she asked, 'Do you want to go to another island?'

'No.' Guy lay back on the picnic rug.

Copying him, Mike tried to empty her mind of everything, relax enough to feel for a few precious seconds at one with the day. But unwittingly her head turned and her eyes sought the face of the man beside her.

He was lying with his hands behind his head, and although his lashes rested on his cheek she knew he wasn't asleep. An aura of silent watchfulness about him indicated his awareness. A stray beam of sunlight probed through the silver canopy of leaves to alight on his hair, burning across it to bring out the colour hidden within the blackness, flames among embers.

She woke to the sound of his regular breathing, and the heat of his long, elegant body against hers. While they had slept both had shifted position, and although he was still on his back she had moved across until she was lying half on him, her cheek pressed to the wide expanse of his chest, his regular heartbeat thudding in her ears, his arms around her.

A jolt of sensation transfixed Mike. Desire, she thought desperately as it flashed, mindless, intoxicating, through her; it was just desire, purely the private joke of Nature, the basic, mindless magnetism of female for male, man for woman. It was the reason for her dry mouth, for the ache that throbbed through her whenever she looked at him.

In spite of her stealthy withdrawal she woke him; he lifted his heavy lashes to look at her with eyes as dazed and indolent as her body. He knew, she realised sickly, and it amused him that she only had to look at him to want him.

Mike gave up subtlety and tried to jerk away, but his arms tightened around her with uncompromising strength. Struggling, she closed her eyes a second, hoping that the rapid thud of her pulses couldn't be seen in the betraying little hollow in her throat. If she had long hair instead of this ridiculous crop she could have hidden her hot cheeks in it, but she had to brazen it out as best she could.

'This is an unexpected bonus,' he murmured, his eyes glimmering with blue lights, amused, perceptive.

'I'm sorry,' she said hastily. 'I don't know how I got here.'

'I gather you're not in the habit of draping yourself over stray sleepers. Pity. I rather like it.'

He was teasing her, and, although she drew a relieved breath when he let her go, she was abruptly, obscurely angry at the light, almost avuncular tone of his voice. She didn't want Guy to feel avuncular; something primal in her wanted him to be as lost to desperation as she was.

CHAPTER FOUR

EDGY and cautious, Mike said, 'I'll finish repacking the hamper.'

'Good idea. Do you need any help?' Guy's voice was uninflected.

'No.' She needed time to regroup her defences, to regain what composure she could. This was getting out of hand, and she didn't know how to deal with it, but the mundane work of tidying up would give her a brief respite.

'Here's one that's trying to get away,' Guy said lazily. He picked a glass up from the sand and leaned over to put it into the hamper.

Mike said, 'I'll do it; I know where it goes,' and went to take it from him. Unfortunately she overbalanced. For a wild moment her arms flailed as she tried to keep herself upright, but inevitably she collapsed—right on to the lean length of his body.

'I'm sorry,' she gabbled, pushing at his sun-heated shoulders, shocked at the tension and hardness beneath her fingers. She knew exactly what was happening to him, for she felt a quickening stir of desire pulse through her.

His mouth curved into a humourless smile. 'So am I. I wonder if it's fate.'

'No,' she gasped wildly, mesmerised by the clear, burning colour of his eyes, lit from behind by some unholy flame.

'Yes.' One masterful hand behind her head pulled her face down to within a hair's breadth of his mouth. His breath tickled her far too sensitive lips. 'I've been trying to avoid this since I saw you, but fate must have it in for me.'

His mouth was firm and insistent. After a first moment of resistance she yielded to it, locked into a pattern she was unable to defy, a pattern of surrender and need, of demand and hunger.

The kiss burned deep into her soul; it comprised the sweetness of grapes, dusky with bloom and promise, and the intoxication of champagne. It was ruthless, exacting, unsparing. And somewhere in the dim reaches of a mind gone crazy, Mike discerned that he was as astonished as she was by its heated fierceness.

Sensation roared through her body, smashing through every barrier she had constructed, until she sighed her angry submission into his mouth, her small slenderness moulding itself to his lithe, taut frame.

When at last he released her Mike couldn't lift her head; she let her face sink down on to his shoulder, shaking with reaction, her hips still moving in involuntary provocation, her breasts so sensitised that the soft cotton between them and his skin seemed an unbearable intrusion.

His chest rose and fell as he dragged air into lungs too long starved of it. He said, 'Dear God,' in a raw whisper, and turned so that she was caged beneath him, prisoner of his body and her own weakness.

The world spun; she must have cried out because he said, 'Hush, sweetheart,' and then he kissed her once more, and it began all over again, the intolerable hunger that grew and grew with each kiss, the merciless impact of his masculinity on her senses robbing her of energy, feeding on her femininity.

'Circe,' he said unevenly against her lips, 'Calypso; you're another nymph on another island, a bewitching, dangerous enchantress, holding my soul to ransom with your black hair and your passionate mouth and your eyes like wild, pale gems. If I kiss you again I might become hooked, but I'm going to.'

This kiss was merciless, as though he was trying to brand her. Mike's heart beat suffocatingly high in her throat; she heard a whimper, and realised that it came from her, and then he thrust his hips into the notch of her body and at the same time his tongue plunged deep, and for a moment she thought she was going to die of wanting.

But he lifted his head, saying roughly, 'Someone's coming.'

Mike opened dazed, silvery eyes.

'Get up,' he commanded, levering himself up from the ground. He extended a hand, pulling her up with such casual lack of effort that she realised anew how very strong he was. As he let her go he said savagely, 'I must be mad.'

Voices galvanised Mike into action. Racked by thwarted passion, eaten up by it, she made herself stuff the last glass into the hamper as Guy shook sand from the rug and folded it.

A quick glance along the beach revealed that the three intruders had stopped and were now crouched down, peering at something in the sand. Mike used the respite granted to exhale deeply, coaxing her frustrated body back from the precipice of a moment ago into some sort of equilibrium.

'We'd better get back to the boat,' she muttered.

He took the hamper from her nerveless grip, smiling with a cold irony that chilled her right through. 'Yes. It's past time to go.'

Once in the boat Mike opened the throttle, burning off the edges of the waves as the little boat jumped from one to the next. In less time than she had ever done the trip before they were back at the wharf. Neither had spoken, but as they got out of the cruiser he said, 'I'm sorry; I shouldn't have kissed you like that.'

Her shoulders moved uncomfortably beneath the cotton of her shirt, but she was not going to let him see just how shattered she was. 'I don't recollect pleading with you to stop,' she returned, trying very hard to project the right amount of airy nonchalance.

He scrutinised her with narrowed eyes. 'You're an intriguing mixture of composure and unexpected shyness. I wonder which is the real Mike—a consummate little flirt, or a shy nymph?'

Something in his tone made her stiffen and glance suspiciously up, but there was no sign of emotion in the angular features. How had he learned to keep such command of his face, of his body language?

Except when a woman fell into his lap, Mike thought wearily. And she couldn't blame him for that. All men were susceptible to open provocation.

'Come on,' he said, taking the hamper from the wharf. 'Let's go back.'

Halfway along the warm, splintery timber he looked around and said suddenly in a voice that was hard and contemptuous, 'This place is a wreck!'

'It's not meant to be a swept-up place like the big new motels over on the Paihia side,' she retorted, angry with him for making her see it through his eyes.

For Far Winds was scruffy, its unkempt buildings and grounds a blatant contrast to the magnificent natural beauty of its surroundings.

'There's no need for the owner to run it into the ground. It doesn't look as though anything's been spent on it since he got here.'

'Harry loves Far Winds,' Mike said defensively.

'He has a strange way of showing it. This looks like exploitation.'

She bit her lip. It was impossible to explain Harry— all laid-back charm, every cent he earned dribbling away on a thousand good causes—to this man, whose every movement expressed a hard-edged energy that was formidable and intimidating. To Harry the buildings were only a necessary evil; it was the Bay he loved, the Bay he introduced his guests to.

Or used to. The Harry of the last three months was a beaten man, slowly drinking his way into uselessness.

As she walked up the path beside Guy, Mike was assailed by two conflicting desires: to remember every second of her time with him, and to pull away. Common sense warned her that in spite of the passion of his kisses he wasn't looking for anything more than a light holiday romance, and she knew better than to indulge in that sort of thing.

Yachts and craft of all kind were heading in towards the inner anchorages; the day of silver and gold and blue was almost over, and Mike, for one, was devoutly thankful for it. Guy's touch, his kisses, were becoming addictive. She had spent the afternoon waiting hopefully for one or both, and she was sickened by her eager, pathetic response to his potent sexuality.

'I'll see you around,' she said, a sudden harsh note charging the words with significance.

There was a moment's silence, not the silence that should fall naturally at the end of a pleasant day out, but one resonating with the unfulfilled emptiness of things left undone.

The winged black brows pulled together in a slight frown, but his voice was unemotional as he said, 'Thank you for the day.'

Mike returned calmly, 'There's no need to thank me. You paid for it.' It sounded churlish, but she didn't care. Smiling, her eyes straying no higher than his beautifully chiselled mouth, she ended coolly, 'I hope it was what you wanted.'

'Yes,' he said. 'It was.'

She was relieved when they got to the main building. 'I'll take the hamper back,' she said in the foyer, holding out her hand for it, eager to be free of his presence.

He took up far too much room in the world. A familiar edginess rubbed her nerves raw. Now that she knew what he tasted like, now that the memory of his body against her was imprinted in her brain, now that she had experienced the exquisite sensations he could summon deep inside her, heat and flame and a narcotic sweetness, she was unable to cope with the sensual overload.

This, she thought roughly, must have been how her mother had felt. And remember where that got her!

He didn't answer, and she looked up. His eyes captured hers, his expression focused, the dark planes of his face purely male, intent and aware.

Excitement licked through every cell in Mike's body.

Ruthlessly she quashed it. After all, it was only physical, and without the fuel of his presence to feed on it would burn out.

'I'll take the hamper back,' she repeated, trying to sound professional and efficient and impersonal.

His smile was crooked. 'All right, then. See you later, Mike.'

It was the casual, all-purpose farewell she'd probably heard ten thousand times, so why should it hurt when he said it?

Because you want more, she told herself viciously as she turned away. Because you are a fool.

That evening there was a *hangi* on the beach, a meal cooked in an earth oven in the way of the Maori before electricity came. Afterwards the local school Maori group would sing songs and dance, and one of the old *kaumatua* of the *marae* would tell a legend about the Bay of Islands, first in his forefathers' language with its magnificent oratory, then in English. Mike loved listening to the Maori words flow through the warm air, and watching the firelight flicker on the wise old face carved by time and experience.

So although officially off duty, she wandered down to the beach at the time when everyone was licking their fingers and complaining of being too full, and found herself a shadowed nook in the shade of one of the pohutukawa trees.

'What are you thinking?'

Guy had appeared so silently that she almost flinched away. He sat down beside her and turned his head so that he could see her face.

'I was thinking that the culture group is a fair cross-section of New Zealand today,' Mike said softly.

His eyes followed hers, inspecting heads all shades of blonde to black, skins every tone from pale Celtic transparency to warm golden brown, eyes that ranged in colour from blue through green and hazel to darkest brown, and features that could have sprung straight from one of the magnificent Polynesian colonising canoes of over a thousand years ago, or the settlers' ships that had come from Europe in the last century.

'Yes,' Guy said slowly. 'We have problems—what country doesn't?—but a group like that is both the hope and the future together.'

At that moment Hohepa got to his feet and began to talk, reeling in his audience with ineffable skill. Guy listened intently, as though he understood the Maori words.

Hohepa's voice rose and fell until, with the instincts of a true actor, he paused, before a last dramatic sentence rolled out in bloodthirsty effect. For a taut moment the only sound was the quiet murmur of the little waves, until the culture group sprang to their feet and, with the young men displaying themselves in the fierce, war-like postures of the *haka*, they retold the legend in dance and song.

The *haka* ended with a blood-curdling yell and a magnificent leap high in the air. Smoothly picking up the slack, Hohepa slid into English and told the same story. Something of a showman, in the best sense of the word, from the first word he had held the audience, young and boisterous as many of them were, firmly in the hollow of his gnarled old hand.

Mike didn't notice. She sat quietly, so acutely conscious of the man beside her that she thought her skin might burst with awareness.

Applause burst out across the water, silvered now by a moon track. The group flocked around the school group, and in a very short time there were impromptu lessons in *haka* movements and the art of twirling the tiny balls called *poi* on the end of their long flax strings. Hohepa's laugh boomed out.

Two people drifted along the beach, recognised Guy, and sat down, smiling greetings. Mike began to get to her feet, but Guy said softly, 'Don't go yet.'

Because some unregenerate part of her heart longed to stay, she obeyed its dictates. Within a few minutes they were discussing the evening show, asking questions, listening intently as Mike answered them. The man was an Australian, big and burly and slow-talking, the woman from Cardiff, in Wales.

Mike enjoyed that first part. It was when the conversation drifted, became more general, that she began to feel uncomfortable. These people had travelled; they were intelligent, aware, and they had some provocative things to say about each country they'd seen. Then they turned to films, to books, to shows. She felt like some ignorant country bumpkin.

How she envied them for being able to initiate an erudite dissection of a book by an up-and-coming writer! She loved reading, but since she had left school she had done very little. Even then, she had known nothing about the books they discussed. Loving Dickens didn't have the same cachet as talking about infinitely esoteric modern writers.

At last she got to her feet with a smile, said, 'Goodnight; no, don't move, enjoy the evening,' and left them to it. Someone had begun to strum a guitar, and songs from all over the world were being requested.

Mike had never felt so lonely in all her life.

That night she dreamed again of Guy's kisses, and progressed to more explicit dreams, dreams that left her with a shattering conviction that she did not know herself nearly as well as she thought she did. She woke just before dawn, sticky and hot, her body aching, her mouth parched.

Dazed by the heavy humidity and the shimmer of moonlight out in the garden, she obsessively recalled the moments she had spent in Guy's arms, feeling her body spring to life instantly, the heat and the need begin to build again.

There could be no future for them; the previous evening had been very revealing. He'd spoken of cities that were only names to her—Rome, London, New York, Paris—and it was clear he knew them well, had friends in all of them. He was cosmopolitan, worldly in the real sense, a citizen of the world, whereas she had only ever been once to Auckland.

A country girl, she thought with a wry, sad smile, with country interests.

Although Guy might be attracted, he wasn't going to fall in love with her. She had nothing to offer him. So she wouldn't be silly and lose her heart to him.

Anyway, he'd be gone soon, taking with him the glamour of his personality.

But when she was racing towards the kitchen an hour later, and he materialised from somewhere to say crisply, 'I want to take you out tonight,' all her good resolutions went sky high.

Mike knew her jaw dropped; she could feel it go. It took a conscious effort of will to press her lips together again, and when that was done she couldn't speak.

He laughed, his blue eyes dancing. 'For dinner,' he said calmly.

'Here?'

He frowned. 'No, not here. I'll get a boat and we'll go to one of the restaurants on the mainland.'

She should say no, but more than anything else she wanted to spend an evening with him. It would be, she realised with a glimmering excitement, the first time she had ever gone out with a man for the evening. 'Yes,' she said simply. 'I'd like that.'

'Good. It has to be tonight because I'm leaving to-morrow,' he said, in a tone so casual she realised it meant nothing to him.

Swiftly, so swiftly that he couldn't see how close her heart was to cracking apart, she asked, 'What time should I be ready?'

'I'll call for you at seven.'

Fortunately she had to work a full eight hours, which took her mind slightly away from the fever of antici-pation that racked her. However much she ordered herself to be practical, she couldn't help wondering whether perhaps this was not the end, but a beginning.

For once she wished she owned a wardrobe of ex-quisite clothes, but beggars couldn't be choosers, she told herself with grim humour. She decided to wear a white lace waistcoat over a white cheesecloth skirt that she had bought for the last end-of-year social at school.

But when she had it on, she wondered whether it was entirely suitable. There seemed to be an awful lot of gleaming olive skin above the white lace. There wasn't anything she could do about her bare shoulders, but to fill in the neck she wore a silver waterfall necklace her mother had treasured.

Her worried eyes scanned the front of the lace waistcoat. She squinted in the mirror, raising and low-ering her arms to see whether her cotton bra showed. No, the tiny pearl buttons in their embroidered loops hid everything.

Not that Guy would spend the evening leering in the hope that some small part of her bra might be revealed! The idea was ludicrous, even if it did make her nipples feel odd and full. Guy was far too urbane to indulge in that sort of adolescent behaviour.

Relieved, she slid her feet into white sandals with medium heels that gave her a little more height. In spite of the heat she should probably wear stockings. However, she didn't possess any. Anyway, her legs were smooth and glossy, polished by summer.

She eyed herself in the mirror, noting the colour that curled along wide cheekbones, the feverish glitter transforming her eyes into silver-blue stars. Lipstick, she thought worriedly, made her mouth seem fuller and softer than ever before, but, short of going without, there was nothing she could do about that.

It would be nice to wear perfume, something modern and haunting with a subtle, erotic undernote that in years to come would bring her vividly to mind whenever it drifted across Guy's nostrils.

Smiling mockingly at herself in the mirror, she applied the pretty lavender fragrance her mother had given her the last Christmas they had spent together.

She was at the gate, smelling one of the old-fashioned roses Linda adored, when he came striding past the selection of old army huts that were the staff quarters.

'You're such a pretty thing,' he murmured, picking the flower with one twist of his fingers and tucking it between the top two saucy pearl buttons. 'There, that sets off your dress perfectly. The Bay Vista was recommended, so I've booked there for us. Have you been there before?'

'No.' It was the best restaurant in the Bay; Mike had heard that it was the most expensive, too. But just then she wouldn't have cared if he'd been taking her to the Ritz. She was still trembling inwardly at the touch of firm, cool fingers pressed for a shivering moment against her suddenly sensitive breasts.

'Well, we'll see what it's like.'

There was something different about him, a tension that transformed the sheen of his eyes into a gleaming brilliance, blue as the heart of a flame, when his gaze lingered on her mouth for a taut, charged second.

Anticipation consumed Mike in a heated rush. 'What time are we due there?' she asked huskily.

'In half an hour, so we'd better get going.'

As they walked through the hotel grounds Mike looked down at the soft lace of her waistcoat, wondering whether it was elegant enough for the occasion. Guy was wearing grey trousers, superbly cut to make the most of his strongly muscled thighs and long legs, a white silk shirt with a muted tie, and a reefer jacket, its subtle nautical shaping entirely suitable. He looked—he looked a man who knew how to handle himself in any situation, a man whose confidence was founded on more solid attributes than the cut of his clothes.

It was no use worrying about her outfit now; it was the best she had, and she wasn't going to spoil the evening by dithering over her clothes. She had done that all day. This was an evening out of time, and she was going to relax and enjoy herself, pretend just for tonight that she did this all the time, went out to dinner with a man she was half in love with.

The Bay Vista lived up to its reputation. The food was superb and the ambience everything she expected, at once polished and cosmopolitan, yet with enough of the Bay's casual style to fit into its surroundings. Guy was attentive without being flirtatious, putting Mike so much at ease that she became able to enjoy the food and the wine and the atmosphere without constraint. Soon she was talking as though she had known him all her life. Although they had almost nothing in common, there was a basic communion of minds that bridged the differences between them.

Clearly, he was accustomed to this sort of entertaining. The waiter deferred to him, he discussed wine intelligently without being obsessed with vintages, and in some subtle manner he dominated the room.

Stimulated by the man and the occasion, Mike allowed her naturally dry wit to surface. He didn't steer the conversation into areas where her lack of experience would be revealed; he made her laugh, and he made her feel she was more than holding her own.

Afterwards, when the evening was over, she would realise that although he didn't give the impression of being particularly sensitive he must have understood exactly how she had felt the previous night, listening to the others talking about topics she was unable to discuss. But that embarrassment came later.

Over coffee Guy asked idly, 'Have you ever thought of leaving the island?'

Until his arrival Mike hadn't realised that for some time she'd been chafing at the restrictions of her life on Far Winds. 'It's not quite that simple,' she said slowly, looking down at her capable, suntanned hand on the peach linen tablecloth. 'I can't just pack up and go.'

'Why not? You must know you're wasting your time there.'

'Things are not going too well for Harry at the moment,' she said warily. 'I'll stay until he gets himself into order.'

'What's the matter?'

Mike sipped coffee, enjoying the intensely fragrant brew. She wanted to look at Guy, but she had been doing that for most of the evening, so she let her gaze wander around the room, noting with what she feared was a certain smugness that many of the women had their eyes fixed on Guy's handsome face. 'I don't know.'

'How long do you think he's going to take to get himself in order?'

Mike shook her head. She hadn't finished the last glass of wine, and the light gleamed ruby in the crystal glass. 'I don't know that, either.'

'Or is Harry just an excuse? Are you afraid of leaving Far Winds, Mike?'

'I haven't exactly got much in the way of qualifications to earn a living,' she said bluntly. 'I suppose I am afraid, a bit.'

He looked at her. 'Why? You can cook for a hotel full of hungry guests, run the same hotel, do the housekeeping and, as far as I can see, all the accounts too. Have you ever thought of going into hotel administration? It's an ever expanding field, and once you're qualified you can travel all around the world.'

She smiled a little cynically. 'But first you have to be trained, and that costs a packet.'

'Can't you get the money?'

'Not a hope. Not unless a charitable millionaire falls in love with me,' she said lightly.

'You could sell your section.'

She shook her head. 'It belonged to my grandparents. I won't be selling it.'

He drank some coffee, his eyes very cool and assessing over the rim of the cup. 'Is Harry your father, Mike?'

Her eyes flew up to meet his, sheer shock dilating them. '*Harry*?' she croaked. 'Don't be silly. Where did you get that idea?'

'Oh, there are a few stray rumours floating around. I wondered.'

She put her cup down with a small crash. 'Harry wasn't even in New Zealand when I was conceived.'

'Who was your father, then?'

Anger made her unwise. Showing her small white teeth in a smile that was a tigerish challenge, she said, 'He was a summer visitor to Russell the year my mother turned eighteen. He wooed her and seduced her, and then he left her. When she told him she was pregnant he said that was tough, because he was already married, and he couldn't afford to support her brat.'

Guy nodded, his expression sympathetic. 'It's an old story, but one that never fails to leave a nasty taste in the mouth. So we both come from what they now call a disfunctional family. Sounds more impressive than a broken home, doesn't it?'

Her brows shot up.

'My parents married, they even loved each other, but they couldn't live together. My father is a farmer,' he said in answer to her unspoken question. A wry smile twisted his chiselled mouth. 'My mother is the spoiled only daughter of a man who never stinted her. She couldn't settle to life in the back of beyond, and Dad wouldn't give up the farm he loved. I don't know what made them think they could make a go of it. They were so different; their marriage was doomed from the start.'

If his father looked anything like Guy, she could understand his mother's behaviour.

'Where are they now?' she asked softly.

'My mother is married to a businessman in Vancouver; they've got two daughters. My father is still on his farm. He married again, too, a woman who grew up in the country. They have a son who is going to take the farm over when he dies. Both Mother and Dad are far happier now than they were when they were married to each other.'

At that moment a band struck up, and he held out his hand. 'Come and dance with me,' he commanded.

This was far from the cheerful country style they had danced to at Far Winds; this band played soft, bluesy music, sophisticated and smooth. Guy's arm held Mike's pliant, slender form close against him. She didn't protest. He was leaving tomorrow, so with half-closed eyes she followed his steps, lost in a dream.

'You move like silk,' he said after a while. 'That's the first thing I noticed about you. You came down the wharf at a run, tossed a comment to the two men who were standing on the pontoon, and floated over into the wheelhouse. I couldn't believe my eyes.'

Shyness made her dumb.

'And then we danced together,' he went on, 'and it was like holding one of the Graces in my arms. Did you have ballet lessons?'

'No.' There hadn't been money for that sort of thing. 'We did gymnastics at school.'

'Just naturally graceful.' His voice was dark and deep, loaded with charm.

Swift little shudders ran through Mike, tiny chills that set her nerves tingling. How could a voice, a certain look, a faint male scent do this to her? She shivered, and his hand tightened.

'Are you cold?'

'No.' Her voice sounded husky, almost raw, yet whispery with it. This, no doubt, was how her mother had felt with the man who had seduced her and then left her.

She stiffened, but his grip kept her against him. 'No, don't pull away,' he said. 'Just for tonight, Mike, let's dance like this.'

So she forgot about tomorrow, forgot about the nasty little piece of gossip he'd relayed to her, forgot about everything but the rapture of being held close enough to him to feel his heartbeat.

The evening was a time of enchantment that didn't finish when they sped back to the island in the runabout, because a moon-path shimmered silver before them all the way. Far Winds was quiet apart from a group making a night of it in the bar; Guy's arm about Mike kept her warm, and when they got back to her front door he said softly, 'Dear little Mike...' and kissed her, first her mouth, then her trembling lashes, then the satin skin of her shoulders.

His mouth was gentle. 'Goodbye, Mike,' he said quietly, and walked away from her and out of her life.

By the time she got to work the next morning he had gone, leaving at seven in the water taxi according to Nola, who wanted to talk a little about him.

Mike couldn't. Whenever his name came up in conversation she suffered a tightness in her throat that blocked her speech. Grief and forlornness gnawed at her.

Of course it would get better.

Only it didn't. She still worried about Harry and his drinking, still ran herself ragged trying to keep the hotel on an even keel, but there was a transparent wall between her and the rest of the world, a screen that imprisoned her in a blank grey misery.

It will pass, she told herself, and made a determined effort to overcome her grief. Her mother had often said that if you acted happy you became happy, so Mike found in herself a talent for acting that would have stood her in good stead on the stage. Unfortunately it appeared that her mother had been wrong.

A month passed, then two. Summer slid inexorably into autumn, days that were hot and beautiful, nights of a crisp clarity that sang like a crystal bowl. There was just enough rain to turn the islands and the hills of the mainland green, not enough to make the farmers happy. The summer rush began slowly to ease off.

Mike went about her work with a resolute smile pinned to her lips. She wrote away to a technical institute and discovered that the fees for a hotel management course were far beyond her. Doggedly, she contacted a couple of hotel chains, enquiring about their trainee schemes.

She was waiting for their answers when Harry came into the kitchen one day as she and Nora were getting lunch ready.

'Mike, come with me,' he said.

'Can't it wait? We've got——'

'No, it bloody can't wait!' He turned on his heel and slammed out of the kitchen.

Nora and Mike stared at each other. Harry never swore.

'You'd better go,' Nora said quickly. 'I can do the rest of this. Go on, hurry up.'

Harry was in his flat, staring at a piece of paper with bloodshot eyes.

'What is it?' Mike asked, her gaze following his.

'It's a letter from the lawyers for the Shelgrave Trust. They've refused my bid for the renewal of the lease and they want me out of here in six months.'

Mike sank down into a chair. 'Oh, God,' she breathed.

Harry laughed mirthlessly. 'Exactly.'

'But they can't do that!'

'Oh, yes, they can, no problems.' Shockingly he put his face in his hands. 'They're going to sell the island to Bishops Holdings. You've heard of Bishops, of course. They're into tourism in a big way—hotels, ships, airlines; they've got them all over the world. Well, they sent a representative up to case the joint, and he recommended that they buy it.'

No wonder Harry had been drinking himself into oblivion every night. 'When did this happen?' Mike asked in a steady voice, more to give herself time than for the information.

Harry laughed again, even more discordantly. 'You know him. Apparently he's old man Bishop's grandson. He came up to spy out the lie of the land. It seems strange to send a member of the family—bad business practice. Perhaps he needed a holiday. Or perhaps because he's got a different name they didn't think we'd know. We didn't, either, so they were right.'

'Who was it?' A cold premonition turned Mike's face pasty.

Harry didn't seem to notice. 'Yeah. Have to hand it to him; he was good. I didn't have a clue. I even liked the young bastard. He had a brain on him. I liked talking to him. But he's organised things so that we have to leave Far Winds.'

'Who? *Who* found out?'

'Guy Lorimer! From Bishops Holdings.'

Mike stared at Harry's ravaged face. 'Guy?' she whispered.

'Yes.' His big hands clenched on the table. 'Forbes Bishop, billionaire several times over, is his grandfather.' He made the words an obscenity. 'Guy Lorimer's going to take over the whole kit and caboodle one day; at the moment he's the old man's trouble-shooter. He well and truly played us for fools.'

Mike got to her feet and walked over to the window. She felt sick and old and tired, her aching heart a cold weight in her chest. Guy, she thought. Oh, Guy.

She had fallen into his cruel grip like a baby bird too young to know that the world was full of predators. He had chatted her up, and flirted with her, and used the bewildered response of her body against her.

And then he had left her.

'They're going to tear everything down and build it up from the ground again,' Harry said tiredly. 'Turn it into a very up-market hotel with a golf course and tennis courts and everything. For the Japanese mainly, I suppose. They like golf, don't they? And if they get sick of this one there's the Waitangi and Kerikeri courses just over the water.'

'Is the island big enough for a golf course?'

'Oh, yes, it's big enough. I thought of doing it myself, once, but it would have cost too much.'

'Perhaps they won't get planning permission.' Mike thought about it for a moment, realising that this was a real possibility. In a tone of forced optimism she went on, 'You know how hard it is for that sort of thing here— the conservationists will fight tooth and nail. The only reason you haven't had trouble with Far Winds Hotel is because it's been here so long.'

But Harry was shaking his head. 'They've got it all worked out. I found out from Bill Nelson on the council. They'll install a special sewage system that'll use the little swamp, so absolutely no pollution'll go into the sea, and they've got a programme all worked out for rubbish disposal. They've filed a very impressive resource-management plan. As well, they're working with the government and the conservation people to turn the coastline into a marine reserve, which will bring divers from all over the world—just like the one at Leigh. No, there'll be no objections from the conservationists.'

Oh, God, Mike thought. All angles covered. She had told Guy about Harry's dream, and he had stolen it. She asked quietly, 'What will you do?'

Harry didn't look at her. 'I don't know,' he said heavily. 'At the moment all I can feel is thank God Dodo isn't here. It would have broken her heart to have to leave Far Winds. She loved every inch of the place.'

Harry had always said that he wanted to be buried beside Dodo, up on the hill overlooking the sunrise. It seemed highly unlikely now; flashy tourist resorts didn't take too kindly to graves everywhere, Mike thought, then tamped down on her incipient hysteria.

It would break Harry's heart, too, if he had to leave Far Winds.

Mike made a pot of tea and they drank it silently, both occupied with their own thoughts. Harry had the look of a defeated man, and Mike couldn't think past the searing, crushing ache of betrayal.

'Harry, I'm so sorry,' she said numbly.

He shook his shaggy head. 'Don't worry about it, little Mike. We didn't have a dog's show. He's a young man, but he's already got a reputation for getting what he wants. None of us would have had a show against an expert manipulator like him.'

For a moment his indignation gave some semblance of animation to his features, but all too soon it died.

'I can't believe it,' she said wearily, but she could. It made Guy's behaviour much more understandable. If he had heard early on that she was Harry's daughter he must have thought he'd be able to pump her for information to make his job easier.

No wonder he had taken an interest in her. A sardonic smile curved her trembling mouth. He certainly hadn't been attracted to her. She'd been living in a fool's paradise.

Her mother had used to say, 'Charm is the most indecent quality a man can have. Nobody is immune to it, because it promises us complete attention, and that's what we all want.'

She had been speaking of Mike's father, but her words applied to Guy as well. He had the ability to convince everyone that he was interested only in them; Mike had been dazzled and beguiled, even though she had known in her heart that she had nothing in common with him.

Nothing but a sexuality that had sent her careering off to the stars. Perhaps the women of her family were doomed to fall in love with specious charmers.

At least she hadn't gone to bed with him, she thought savagely, then wondered whether she'd have been able to resist him if she'd possessed information he really needed.

All lies. Oh, he had wanted her, but she had hoped it was special for him, that although she couldn't share his life he would always remember her with a smile and some affection.

Whereas if he remembered her at all it would probably be with a cynical amusement. Those kisses had just been a bonus for him.

Humiliation gripped her, shaking her so that tears came suddenly to her aching eyes. Swine, she thought fiercely.

What on earth were they going to do?

That night as she lay awake, her open eyes fixed unseeingly on the ceiling above, an idea formed in her mind. It was not fair that Guy should be allowed to create such havoc and get away with it. Someone should see to it that he paid.

But how could he be made to pay? He was rich, and powerful, and ruthless.

At the very least he should have it forcibly pointed out to him what he had done to Harry.

Harry wouldn't do it.

Which left only her.

Her whole being rose in revulsion. She could not do it. It would mean going down to Auckland, tracking Guy down, and facing him in his office. If he let her; he might simply inform his secretary not to make an appointment. If he did that, she'd have to find some other way of seeing him, and the mere thought of that made her come out in a cold sweat.

But why should he get away scot-free?

CHAPTER FIVE

THE idea preyed on Mike's mind. She couldn't talk it over with anyone, but it wouldn't have made any difference. Her decision was made seconds after the idea came to her.

At first she wondered whether it was a cover for a sly, shameful need to see Guy again, but the mere thought of that made her shudder. He had used her. There were no excuses for him, no emotion that could stand against that sort of exploitation. The tender shoot of admiration and attraction was frosted and dead.

Three days after he had received the news Harry told the staff. 'I've asked about jobs in the new resort,' he said towards the end of his short speech, 'but there's no joy there, I'm afraid. Bishops train their own staff, they told me, so there'll be no new positions for any of you.'

Until then Mike had been too preoccupied with her own pain to realise more than intellectually what it would do to the rest of the people who worked at the hotel, people who were her friends, but as she saw their faces she understood that this was not just her personal tragedy. It affected them all, and some of them far more deeply than it did her.

The younger ones, those who could travel to find jobs, were the least upset. Nola, who lived with Sean and their two small children in the other staff cottage, was shattered.

Afterwards she said heavily, 'Well, that's that, then. The end of the best six years in my life. It's hard enough to get a job when you're in your twenties, but it's almost impossible once you're over forty.'

'But you're a really good cook,' Mike said, trying to look on the bright side. 'You won't find it hard to get a job. Harry will give you a super reference.'

Nola gave her a speaking look. 'Come on, Mike, I've got no qualifications at all. Before we came here I was just a housewife. Sean was on the dole so we were living in a caravan park in a grotty old house-truck. Meeting Harry and being offered a job here was like tripping over paradise on the way to buy some milk. I don't know what we're going to do now.'

Harry had said that he was closing the hotel in a month. Nola looked desperate, her eyes leached of colour and hope. She said tiredly, 'There won't be any jobs for us in the new Far Winds. They'll want smart young kids who can speak Japanese.'

Sick and furious, Mike looked around and saw the same desperation on other faces. New Zealand was in the grip of a recession, and, in spite of newspaper articles saying that the worst was over and business was picking up again, things were still difficult in Northland, traditionally the region hardest hit by recession. Few jobs were being advertised.

'Just before winter, too,' Nola said drearily. 'What are you going to do, Mike?'

'I don't know.'

But she did know. A conversation later that night only put a seal on the decision she had made.

Harry looked down at the cup of coffee he had doctored with a large tot of brandy, and said, 'I felt so bloody helpless looking around them all. I'll do what I can, but winter's coming up, so no other resorts will be taking on new staff at least until the spring. And there's no way I can pay them redundancy.'

Mike nodded. The taste of coffee bitter in her mouth, she asked, 'What are you going to do?'

'Put a bullet in my brain,' he said.

She shivered. 'Don't be silly.' Her voice was sharp and quick.

He shrugged morosely, staring out of the window at the quiet night. 'Don't worry about me, Mike. What will you do?'

'Oh, I'll find a job,' she said cheerfully. 'I know everyone in the Bay; I won't have any difficulty.'

She would definitely confront Guy. Not that she fooled herself it would do any good—Bishops had, after all, every right to do what they had done—but at the very least she could make Guy Lorimer realise just how many lives he was going to damage. The next day saw her on the morning bus to Auckland.

She had been there once before when she was fifteen, and no one, she thought when the bus finally stopped at the station, could have been more impressed than she was then by the noise and bustle and the number of people. She was almost as intimidated now. But she caught a taxi to the budget hotel where Harry stayed on the rare occasions he came to New Zealand's largest city, and once in her room sat down with the telephone directory.

It was easy to find. Bishop Tourism. For a moment Mike's heart quailed. That entry, with all it implied, revealed just how distant Guy was from her, from all the ordinary people who lost their jobs when big corporations played games. Right from the start she had noticed the invisible but potent aura of power that clung to him. Most of it had been an indication and extension of his natural personality, but that inborn authority could only have been made more formidable by growing up in such an important family.

Who the hell was she to think that she could put any sort of pressure on him?

Her confidence wavered, until something cold and still and silent, something she had never recognised in her character before, insisted she continue. Slinking back home without even trying was unthinkable. Oh, she probably wouldn't be able to make any difference to the ultimate outcome, but at least he should be forced to face just what he had done to everyone at Far Winds, and that wasn't going to happen unless she did it. Setting her jaw, she resumed her search.

She looked for his name and initial in the private numbers, but there was nothing there. What she'd do, she finally decided, was ring Bishop Tourism and ask for an appointment with him.

What if they asked why she wanted to see him?

She pushed the frown from between her brows with her first three fingers. What had seemed so easy in the Bay of Islands suddenly was fraught with pitfalls. She could say it was about Far Winds. But if she did that she'd warn him, and he might refuse to meet her.

Briefly, she considered saying she wished to see him on a private matter. Her head lifted and her mouth tightened as pride vetoed that; he might think she was chasing him.

So she would have to say it was business, and if the secretary or receptionist or whoever asked for more she would simply repeat her request firmly, and add that it was important.

In case she got tongue-tied she wrote down what she wanted to say. Thus armed, she dialled the number. Fear and a kind of uneasy anticipation were mixed with outrage and a bitter sense of betrayal to make a volatile, unmanageable cocktail of emotions inside her.

It was every bit as embarrassing as she thought it would be. The telephone operator sounded distinctly dubious, the receptionist even more so, but by dint of saying politely and implacably that she needed to see Mr Lorimer she managed to eventually get through to a cool-voiced woman.

This person, after presumably consulting with him, came back and said that Mr Lorimer would see her in half an hour's time.

Sticky with sweat and slightly shaky with reaction, Mike put down the receiver. Still in the jeans and T-shirt she'd travelled in, she wasted ten seconds by opening the wardrobe door and inspecting its contents. The only decent dress she had was crushed, and she didn't have time to press it. Hastily she rang the desk, discovered that it took a taxi probably fifteen minutes to get her to the Bishop office, and asked them to order one immediately. She would have to go as she was. But first she had a quick wash down and scrambled into a fresh T-shirt before applying a coat of lipstick and combing her hair into some sort of order.

Almost exactly half an hour later she was being shown into Guy's office high above the city by an extremely elegant woman in her mid-thirties who, after the first appalled moment, managed to hide her astonishment at Mike's appearance.

Already overwhelmed by the subdued luxury of the huge complex, Mike's face settled into rigid lines.

Guy got to his feet as she came in. In these surroundings he was completely alien, his dark business suit giving him a remoteness that effectively cut him off from the glamorous stranger of the days at Far Winds.

'Thank you, Sheila. Mike,' he said, his eyes very keen as they scanned her features, 'how are you?'

'I'm fine, thank you.' She knew her voice was stony, but if she allowed any emotion to show it would be the sort she couldn't expect him to overlook—hatred and contempt and a stinging despair.

'To what do I owe the pleasure of this visit?' he asked, watching her from beneath half-closed lids.

'I think you owe me something,' she said bleakly. 'After all, you've just put paid to my job.'

He didn't move, but his eyes narrowed further so that all she could see was a burning sliver of colour beneath the thick black lashes. 'When did you hear?'

'Does it matter?' She didn't try to hide the bitterness in her tone.

'Yes, it does,' he said without emotion. 'How did you know who had bought the island? Did the lawyers for the trust tell you?'

'No, their letter just said the island had been sold and gave Harry six months to get out. Harry has a mole in the council and he found that you'd filed for planning permission.'

'I see.'

Mike felt a sudden shaft of fear. She shouldn't have told him that. Hastily she went on, 'Not that that matters, because we'd have known soon enough.'

'What has all this to do with you?' he asked in a voice smooth and bland as cream.

'I came to—to ask what you're going to do.' She hated it, but she couldn't hide the note of pleading in her words.

'That comes under the heading of business, Mike.' His tone was quiet but inflexible.

She bit her lip. As soon as she had walked into his office and seen the stranger standing there she had known she was on a hopeless mission, but she had to make him understand what he was doing. She began again. 'Most of the people who work there haven't got a hope of finding another job. A lot of them are there because Harry's got a kind heart and he felt sorry for them.'

'So what do you expect me to do?'

'You can't just throw them out of work and on to the scrap-heap.' Her voice, her stance, her stormy eyes bespoke her belligerence.

There was a moment's silence, until he said pleasantly, 'I still can't see what you want me to do. If Harry had paid a little more attention to business instead of dreaming the days away on his romantic island he might have been in a better position to look after these workers you say he cares so much about. What about their redundancy payments?'

He read the answer to that in her face. His expression hardened into granite, but when he spoke it was in a dispassionate, deliberate voice that made her take a step back. 'So not only did he get away with paying his staff a pittance, you included, because most of them were so grateful for a job they'd have worked for almost nothing, but he's going to waltz away without paying a cent of redundancy. Perhaps there's something to be said for Harry's brand of philanthropy, after all.'

'You don't know what you're talking about,' she said icily. 'I shouldn't have come here.'

'No, you shouldn't. I'm not a welfare agency, Mike. I'm not responsible for idiots who don't take advantage of the laws the government passes to protect people like them. It's their own fault they find themselves in this position.' He spoke coolly and calmly, without any pretence of compassion.

Mike's heart was breaking, shattering. 'No, you're not a welfare agency; you're a ruthless, callous, cold-hearted beast. I hope your venture fails.'

Something ugly blazed into life in his eyes. 'It won't,' he said softly. 'I don't accept failure.'

She held her ground, but with difficulty. This man was a truly frightening stranger, so different from the man at Far Winds that there seemed no connection between the two. 'Do you know that Harry can't even claim compensation from the trust?'

He laughed mirthlessly. 'Why the hell should he be compensated? What for? He's let the place run down until it's practically falling to bits—in spite of a lease which put the onus on him to maintain the hotel. Because of that proviso he's paid what amounts to a peppercorn rental for the last twenty years, yet he's put nothing away for his old age. Face it, Mike, he may be charming and intelligent and amusing, but he's a manipulator. Ever since he took over Far Winds he's sat back enjoying a life second to none, and done the bare minimum to keep the place going.'

Her smile was bitterly ironic. 'You still don't understand, do you? I don't suppose you've ever met anyone like Harry before. He's a soft touch, a philanthropist in the best sense of the word. There probably isn't anyone around the Bay who hasn't borrowed money from him, and never been dunned to pay it back. He supports children all over the world——'

A lean, upraised hand stopped her. 'Then let the people who owe him money bail him out,' he said curtly. 'For the last ten years he's known that the trust would be more than happy to sell the island. He thought he had them over a barrel because of the recession, and because he'd let the buildings go so far down that it would cost far more than the place was worth to bring it back into paying order. He was sure no one else would ever buy the island or take over the hotel. It was a calculated ploy, Mike, and he lost, fair and square. He can't expect to play with the big boys then cry foul when things don't go the way he wants them to.'

'So for you it's just a matter of business.' She was openly scornful now, so angry that the words came spitting out without hesitation. 'Harry's not like that! He's kind, and generous—all right, he's not the world's best businessman, and he might be foolishly optimistic, but he's not conniving, or an opportunist. Your own ruthlessness has blinded you from seeing the real man. Harry and a lot of the others on Far Winds are getting old, and won't have anything when they leave. What will they do? Where will they go?'

'I neither know nor care. That's Harry's responsibility—something, I might add, he should have thought of in the years when he was letting the hotel moulder into the ground.'

Drawing a deep, painful breath, Mike turned towards the door. 'I knew you were despicable,' she said viciously, 'but I didn't know just how bad you really are.'

His smile showed strong white teeth. 'And you haven't even seen me when I've been trying,' he said, mocking her. 'Given half a chance, I can be much worse than that.'

'I'm sure you can.' She walked across the thick carpet, paid for no doubt by people he had ruined, wondering stonily how on earth she could have been falling in love with a man who rode roughshod over anyone in his way without compunction.

'Of course,' he said, his voice silky and smooth, 'I could be persuaded.'

Mike's head jerked up as though she had been hit on the chin. Freezing, she said in a remote voice, 'To do what?'

'Oh, to see if we can work out some form of redundancy payments, perhaps.'

She didn't dare turn her head. 'Persuaded. By what?'

'Well——' he drew the word out for maximum effect '—how about coming out to dinner with me tonight?'

To her horror Mike realised that she was almost tempted. Sickened by the treachery of her emotions, she said tonelessly, 'I'd rather eat dinner with the wolves at the zoo, thank you.'

'Pity. You wouldn't convince them to do anything for these people you're so worried about, whereas you just might convince me.'

Get going, she commanded herself. Don't listen to the devil tempting you; just put one foot in front of the other and get going out of here and away.

But her foot wouldn't move, and the hand that hadn't quite closed on the door-handle stayed still, not opening it.

'How?' she asked the door.

She couldn't see him, but she heard the smile in his voice. 'You'll just have to see, won't you?'

'No,' she said quietly, intensely. 'I'm not going to be manipulated any more. If you want to make a deal, then tell me what it is.'

'When have I ever manipulated you?'

Turning her head, she looked at him with eyes that were colourless in a colourless face. 'You thought I was Harry's daughter. That's why you—you thought you might learn something from me.'

'You've got it all worked out, haven't you?' he said. No emotion softened the carved symmetry of his face.

'Not that it matters. You aren't Harry's daughter. But if you come out to dinner with me tonight, I'll make sure that some form of redundancy payment is made to the staff.'

Shaking her head, she said scathingly, 'You don't understand. This isn't a matter of a few hundred dollars, for God's sake.'

'I'd have to be deaf and exceedingly thick not to have realised that. You've waxed most eloquent about their plight. I can help them, Mike. I have the power.'

She shivered, the fine hairs on the back of her neck lifting. Yes, he had power; she had felt it when she'd walked into his office; power, naked and unashamed, aggressively edged with steel, used as a weapon.

He was young, but his grandfather was legendary, and Guy was set to follow him. She should tell him to go to hell, but she was unable to do it. Nola's face, gaunt with hopelessness, was hideously clear in her mind.

And anyway, she thought wearily, what did it matter that she loved him as well as despised him, that each moment spent with him was an exquisite torment? Someone might gain something from her pain. Slowly she nodded.

'Where are you staying? I'll pick you up at seven-thirty.' His voice was imperious and arrogant.

In a monotone she gave him the address.

He said curtly, 'That's not a very salubrious area.'

'It's all right. I don't intend to wander the streets at night, and it's clean and comfortable.'

'Is it?' His tone altered as he came closer, turned her stiff, unyielding face with a casual, insulting finger. His gaze dropped disparagingly to her jeans and T-shirt. 'Wear something a little more festive than those clothes, Mike.'

Her chin lifted. Eyes as clear and as hard as diamonds sparkling beneath obstinately lowered lids, she said in a polite, wooden voice, 'Yes, of course. Goodbye.'

He laughed, and cupped her mutinous chin, holding her there while he commanded softly, 'Look at me. Lift those ridiculously long lashes and look at me.'

It took all of her will-power to do it. She sent him a very level, scorching stare, holding his gaze unflinchingly. Something in the dark blue eyes leapt into life, and Mike's lashes fell again.

Guy's muttered curse almost evaded her hearing, but his kiss flooded her skin with heated colour, and she had to bite back a muffled gasp. Her hand came up to rub her mouth as she stared at him.

'You can't escape me,' he said, his hostility nakedly obvious. His hand dropped.

Wide-eyed, her mouth still quivering from that hard kiss, Mike stepped back. Guy touched a button, saying when the door opened behind her, 'Sheila, order a taxi for Ms Christopher, will you? And see that she takes it.'

Which the woman did by escorting Mike down the lift and out through the wide, opulently impressive foyer to the waiting taxi. She seemed pleasant enough, and her conversation was polite. Unfortunately Mike couldn't respond with anything but a shallow courtesy that must have made her sound surly and evasive.

Where was he going to take her for dinner? It was stupid to be worrying about something so trivial when her heart was breaking into jagged fragments in her breast, but by concentrating on her clothes she was almost able to disregard the other. That walk through the building had revealed that the dress she had in her wardrobe was so far from being chic it might just as well be a grass skirt.

No, she thought, common sense reasserting itself as her dazed eyes stared unseeingly at the turmoil of traffic outside, she would not pay out for a dress she didn't need. Her bank balance was in fair shape, but...

She owed it to herself, she thought angrily, to look self-possessed and in full control of the situation. That was a better reason to buy a new dress than her mortifying desire to look less like a hick.

Leaning forwards, she asked the cab driver, 'Where could I buy a nice dress, not too expensive?'

'Plenty of places, love,' the woman said, 'but my girls always go to the Emporium in High Street. You can pick up some great bargains there, and the staff are nice and helpful.'

'Can you drop me off there?'

'Yes, of course I can.'

When they got there Mike went to pay, but the woman laughed. 'No, that's been taken care of, love. Buy yourself a pretty dress, now.'

Persuaded by the assistant, a tiny grasshopper of a girl whose stunning looks were set off perfectly by the clothes she wore, Mike chose a dress of deep hot pink, a deceptively simple little thing in a knitted material that clung to her firm breasts and narrow waist and flared out over her hips. The unexpected colour gave warmth and depth to her olive skin and contrasted dramatically with her black hair and pale eyes. And it was an end of season mark-down at less than it would have taken to make it.

'I knew it'd look great on you,' the salesgirl enthused, eyeing her with a particularly impersonal stare. 'Look, get a lipstick that colour, and eyeshadow in a smoky plum or ash-blue, and you'll knock his eyes out.'

'Shoes,' Mike said helplessly, staring at the vivid, unknown creature in the mirror.

'Black courts. They're having a sale next door. And the woman in the chemist a couple of blocks down is really good for make-up—or go up to Smith and Caughey's and ask one of the women there to give you a face-job. They're excellent.'

Feeling as though she had stepped into a whirlwind, Mike bought a pair of perfectly plain black shoes, elegant and understated and for practically nothing, before making her tentative way to the chemist's shop. She almost turned tail at the sight of the frighteningly attractive woman behind the counter, but a few moments' conversation proved the assistant to be friendly and interested. She suggested some economical cosmetics, showed her how to apply them, and ended by making up her eyes in hues that looked alarming until Mike saw herself in the mirror and gasped at the subtlety of the mixed colours.

'You've got the most amazing eyes,' the woman said admiringly. 'Don't bother with foundation—skin as fresh and young as yours doesn't need it—but I'll put in some blusher, because you haven't really got any colour in your cheeks. This is how you put it on.'

When she finished Mike stared at her reflection with awe and a stirring excitement. Guy would get more than a little shock when he saw her. Something cold and practical told her that this small victory would be one way of asserting herself, of shoving him off balance. He was expecting the ragamuffin he had seen on the island and a few hours ago, but she would show him that she could scrub up with the best of them.

Economical or not, the price of the cosmetics made her blench. Setting her teeth, she paid up, and, with her parcels in a carrier-bag, headed towards the bus-stop.

Ready ten minutes before Guy was due, she spent the time giving herself a pep talk, trying to convince herself that she would treat him with a mixture of aloofness and caution. She wasn't going to let his overwhelming charisma obscure the fact that he had used her, then compounded his sin by ruthlessly blackmailing her into going out with him. All she had to do was remember—and keep remembering—that he was callous and unscrupulous, and totally lacking in compassion or kindness.

She would show him that she was not so easily intimidated by his wealth, and his position. She would show him that she despised him.

When he came in she was sitting very straight in a chair in the small, spotless lobby, pretending to read a magazine. At the sight of him in a well-cut dinner-jacket her heart thudded. In spite of her caution a sizzle of excitement and determination lit her eyes into huge, pale blue jewels. Thank heavens she had given in to temptation to buy a new dress!

But with the excitement came an icy pragmatism.

Why had such a man, with all his attributes, power, social position, fascinating personality and the effortless masculine virility that marked him out from all other men, why should such a man have blackmailed her into going out with him?

The answer, of course, was obvious, and unpleasant.

Because she had defied him, made him realise just how much she despised him. A man who had been brought up to believe that whatever he wanted, whatever he did, was right, a man like Guy, would turn arrogant and vengeful when confronted by another's disdain.

So he had hit back.

Not, she thought sturdily as she got to her feet, that she cared. As long as she remembered Harry and Nola and all the others who worked at the hotel, Guy's untrammelled masculinity wouldn't be able to get to her; she could fight the promptings of her treacherous body.

Guy glanced quickly around the small lobby, his thoughts apparent although his expression didn't change. It didn't change when she got to her feet, either, but she sensed his appreciation immediately.

'You look delicious,' he said softly. 'Far too pretty for a place like this.'

Mike's brows lifted. 'It's clean, and it's cheap,' she said, adding pointedly, 'Harry recommended it.'

Something moved in the depths of his eyes, but his smile didn't alter. 'Did he?' he said, and kissed her, lifting his head to watch with unkind amusement the tide of colour that scorched up through her skin. 'Let's go.'

He was driving a sports car, an E-Type Jaguar. A young man's car, Mike thought, trying to be scornful—a flagrant, unashamed symbol of masculinity. He drove competently and swiftly through the grey cityscape towards the waterfront, pulling into an underground car park beneath an old but newly renovated building.

'Where are we going?' she asked tentatively when he opened the door for her to get out.

He smiled obliquely and took her arm. 'Oh, somewhere with a view of the sea. I wouldn't want you to get homesick.'

A lift, small but luxuriously appointed, shot them up the five or six floors to a carpeted hallway. It didn't need a sight of the obviously private hall for Mike to understand that he had brought her to his apartment.

Words clogged her throat, choking on the barrier of her anger and a hidden, unacknowledged anticipation that pulsed beneath.

'There,' he said, indicating the windows. 'In its own way as beautiful as the view from Far Winds, I think.'

The harbour was bathed in the afterglow of a sunset that still incarnadined the sky behind the Waitakere ranges. On the left the arc of the bridge glowed with lights against bush-clad hills. Rangitoto loomed to the north, its triple cone darkly ominous against the flushed sky. The waters of the harbour gleamed like molten metal, and all around the lights of the city glittered and sparkled in a fairy-tale beauty, bewitching, glamorous, hiding the sometimes dingy daytime reality of the streets and docks. A freighter was moving slowly down the channel towards the wharfs below.

Mike said quietly, 'It's beautiful. But you can't hear the water. Or the birds.'

'No. This is Auckland, after all.' His voice altered. 'Shall we forget why you're here, Mike, and pretend a little? We enjoyed each other's company before. Why shouldn't we do that now?'

He stood behind her. In the window she could see their silhouettes, her small one, his much larger, almost obscuring her. It would be so easy to give in.

'I'm sorry,' she said harshly, 'but I haven't such a convenient memory. I'm not here because we enjoyed each other's company, but because you said that if I came you'd help Harry and the staff. That's all.'

He laughed deep in his throat. 'Very well, then. What would you like to drink?'

'Orange juice,' she said quickly.

'Oh, I think you can branch out. I'll open some champagne and you can see how it goes with orange juice.'

Shrugging, she let it go. She wasn't used to alcohol, but he couldn't force her to drink the stuff. From beneath thick lashes she watched while he went across to the small refrigerator in the kitchen and with the minimum amount of fuss opened a bottle of champagne. He was smiling as he brought her back a glass of pale orange liquid, but she discerned deeper, more turbulent emotions beneath the mask of his worldliness.

No, he hadn't forgiven her for her heated, intemperate words in his office. Well, that was all right, because she hadn't forgiven him, either.

'What shall we drink to?' he asked softly. 'I know. To us. May we each get what we deserve in life.'

It was a not too subtle gibe, but Mike pretended to take it at face value, even drinking a small amount of the mixture. It was absolutely delicious, and she said so.

'Buck's fizz. Now, where would you like to go for dinner?' he asked.

Mike shook her head. 'I don't know anywhere,' she said warily, wondering what he was up to.

'I thought you might have heard of a restaurant you'd like to go to. I know a good one. Excuse me for a moment while I reserve a table.'

Had he brought her to his home just to see the view? Or had her obduracy meant a change in plans? If she

hadn't proved immune to his plea for things to be as
they were, would they have had dinner in this luxurious
apartment with its intriguing leather chairs in dark blue
and steel, and the wide, comfortable sofa? The room
was another barrier between them, breathing of money
and urbanity and a cool, refined taste. It wasn't in the
least cosy, she thought, the corners of her mouth tucking
up, but then neither was Guy.

Pretending to look out of the window, Mike sipped a
little more of the buck's fizz. She eyed his reflection in
the glass, the broad back turned to her, shoulders slightly
hunched as he punched in numbers, the long, well-
muscled legs revealed so cleverly by the excellent tail-
oring of his trousers, a strong, elegant hand thrust into
his trouser pocket as soon as he was answered.

Her stomach flipped, sending shock waves of sensation through her entire system. At that moment she
wanted him with an intensity that had something
primitive and barbaric in it. It was more than desire. It
was an implacable hunger, a lightning flash of need.

Was this how her mother had felt with the man who
was her father?

Mike bit her lip until the pain recalled her to her very
real danger, and was only just able to compose her face
by the time Guy turned around. His expression was
watchful, almost amused, yet a hard recklessness showed
for a moment as he let his eyes travel insolently over her
body.

Mike wished that she had worn the dress she had dis-
carded. What on earth had persuaded her to buy this
brilliant outfit? Sheer vanity, and she was paying for it
now. With a hand clenched around the stem of her glass
she waited while he hung up.

'Finish your drink,' he said softly, never taking his
eyes off her, 'and we'll go.'

If Mike had needed any confirmation of his position
in Auckland society she got it when they walked into
the restaurant. It was small, decorated with a quiet good

taste that murmured of an enormous amount of money and thought, and it was full. Unsophisticated Mike knew herself to be, yet she realised it was highly unlikely that just anyone would have been able to reserve a table at such short notice, let alone the secluded one to which the head waiter led them, tucked halfway behind an exquisite Chinese screen.

And if that hadn't been enough, the way they were watched would have revealed it to her. On almost every face there was recognition, and a kind of poised eagerness, as though Guy had only to recognise them to get an effusive reaction.

He did smile and nod to several of the other diners, and their responses were immediate and unguarded. Clearly Guy Lorimer was well-known, and very well respected. Mike ignored the puzzled glances directed at her. She had, she told her aching heart, only a few hours to get through and then she could start to forget him.

The meal was magnificent. Mike chose roast saddle of venison with blackberry sauce, and, by dint of telling herself sternly that she would probably never be able to afford to eat in a restaurant like this again, she forced herself to enjoy the delicious meat in its light, flaky pastry, lingering over the unexpected tastes of chestnuts and juniper berries.

Guy was an intriguing companion. He talked wittily and intelligently of a variety of things; Mike responded with a composure that surprised her. She sipped the red wine he had chosen, and because it didn't matter any more she let herself go a little, challenging him, putting her own point of view with more emphasis than was normal for her.

She expected condescension, but although his eyes gleamed occasionally with a mocking light he didn't patronise her. About halfway through the meal she found that she was enjoying herself. She should have been aghast at such base treachery; instead, she decided defiantly to deal with that aspect of her behaviour tomorrow. Tonight was—an evening out of time.

Tonight was hers. Fairy-story stuff, Cinderella and all that. She would enjoy it. Recriminations could wait.

And she was pleased she had bought the dress, that her eyes glittered and her cheeks glowed, because when he looked at her he liked what he saw, she could tell. She might be almost totally naïve when it came to the relations between the sexes, but in this arena instinct was more important than experience, and for all his sophistication Guy couldn't hide his primal response to her.

'It's too early to go home,' he said when it was over.

Mike said on a note of surprise, 'It's eleven o'clock.'

'I know. Far too early.' Restlessness coloured his tones. 'I know where we'll go.'

It was a nightclub. At first Mike was disappointed, because it was noisy, and there was no way they could talk, but she soon realised that there were other compensations. Dancing, she thought an hour later, drunk on his presence, dazzled by his lean, warm body, the faint, infinitely arousing scent of his masculinity, was like making love to music.

She had ascended to another plane of existence, where her senses were infinitely expanded, her capacity for pleasure, for excitement, stretched unbearably. They hadn't talked much, just danced until the music had somehow blended with her physical tiredness and mental exhaustion so that she was lost to her ordinary self.

'Tomorrow,' she whispered, but as an incantation it had lost its power.

'Let's go,' Guy said abruptly.

She went with him docilely, walking out into the enchanted streets of an unknown city, smiling, her small face vivid with emotions she no longer bothered to conceal. When Guy caught her hand she let it lie unresisting in the warm strength of his. The sound of their steps on the footpath was a measured counterpoint to the rapid beating of her heart.

Once in the car he put the key in the starter motor, but looked across at her before he turned it. Mike smiled, and he said with difficulty, 'Don't look at me like that.'

Delight exploded through her. 'Like what?' she asked, conscious that her voice was slow and lethargic.

'As though you feel the way I do.' His words were oddly slurred, yet like her he had drunk only a glass of champagne and one of the superb red wine over dinner.

'And how is that?'

Eyes glittering strangely in his hard face, he said unhurriedly, 'Caught in a spell. Lost in a fairy-tale.'

'Yes,' she agreed, her smile ripe with promise. 'That's exactly how I feel.'

He gave a kind of groan, and reached across to pull her into his lap. Mike touched his cheek, and his mouth crushed down on her soft lips in a kiss that seared through the last of her resistance, setting her aflame with the desire she had been fighting all evening.

He lifted his head, but only to mutter a few shaken, wondering words. Mike kissed the angle of his jaw, and his hand speared the tangle of her curls, pulling her head back so that he could taste along the line of her neck.

After a while he said, 'We have to get out of here,' and put her back in her seat, running his hand through his hair.

He took her to his apartment. Neither spoke as they went up in the lift, nor when he unlocked the door and shut it behind them. Immediately his arms closed around her, and without any thought of opposition she lifted her face invitingly.

He kissed her with the intensity of a starving man, in an agony of hunger. Mike responded with a similar passionate ferocity, asking nothing more of life than this moment. Her mouth opened beneath the demand of his as passion soothed her inchoate fears with the savage insistence of rapture, until at last they were in his huge, shadowy bedroom and he was removing the bright dress from her willing body so that his mouth could find the pleading aureole in her breast.

Mike cried out, her small, competent hands ruthless as they ripped his shirt open, then spread wide over his chest, trying to soak in the potent masculinity.

'Mike,' he said in a thick, impeded voice against her breast. 'Little witch, with your lush red mouth and those wild, pale eyes...'

He lifted her high against his heart and carried her across to the wide bed, putting her down before tearing himself free of his clothes to follow her. Mike watched with lazy, slumbrous eyes. She should have been shocked, frightened even, at the rampant masculinity, the explicit promise of his sleek, bronzed body.

Instead she felt the fires of desire and need coalesce, become a raging inferno she could no longer control. She struggled up to undo her bra, but he said, 'No, let me,' and slipped the fragile thing free, so that she was lying in her briefs and tights.

His hands on her skin were experienced and sure, yet they trembled when he touched her, and there was something reverent, almost awed, as he traced the softly feminine contours of her body. 'You dazzle my eyes,' he said harshly. 'You bewitch me. I feel like Apollo when he saw Daphne on the riverbank and was lost.'

Mike pressed her palm to the centre of his chest, feeling the thud of his heart drive into it. She took his hand and held it over hers, and like that, looking so intensely into each other's eyes that Mike thought he must surely see her soul, they stayed until, compelled by a strange linkage, their heartbeats synchronised.

'Mike,' he whispered. 'Oh, God, darling...'

His mouth crushed hers, explored the depths that opened so compliantly to him with a driven determination that summoned a like intensity in her. Then he made a necklace of kisses, dropping the pendant between her breasts.

At the crushed-silk brush of his beard against her sensitive skin, she drew a sobbing breath, her slender body arching imperatively against the sleek hardness of his, demanding an invasion she barely understood.

'No,' he said, a feral smile stretching his lips, 'not yet, you tantalising little nymph.'

His mouth on her breast was slow and erotic and tormenting, sending fierce waves of delight through her until she grabbed his hair and pulled him away, shaking so hard that she couldn't articulate the words she needed.

'Yes,' he murmured, 'you like that, don't you? But you're right, there are other ways to drive us both to heaven.'

He showed her some of them. He touched her with devastating skill, with fiery demands and tenderness, with a knowledgeable expertise that melted her bones. Mike knew the technicalities of making love. She had read books where it was graphically, even sensuously described, but she had never realised her body could experience such sensations that she lost the quick intelligence she was justly proud of and became what she had always despised, a woman with nothing but need to drive her actions, at the mercy of her body, of a hunger that was at once splendid and terrifying, rapturous and forbidding.

Those gasping little moans came from her throat, the hands that stroked across his skin, exploring at first gingerly then at his shuddering encouragement with increasing confidence, were hers, the lips that tasted salt on his skin, learned the contours of his magnificent body in a new and exciting way, were hers.

When she thought she might die of hunger, when her body was strung tight as a bent bow, when she could say nothing but soft, broken, pleading words, he laughed the hard, fierce laugh of a lover, and with one thrust of his body took what she offered so openly, so freely.

Her mother had warned that it might hurt, but there was no pain. When he slid home as though she had been made for him, instinct told her what to do. Her hips rotated reflexively, welcoming him in, taking him inside her.

His chest lifted as he dragged air into his lungs; Mike felt the mighty tremor that rolled through him, and realised that he was just as affected as she. Awe and delight mingled deep inside her. He had seemed so different from her, so opposed in every way, yet here, on this bed, they lay locked together as equals, both taking, both giving, both snared in a sensual spell that bound them together in a place where no one else dared intrude.

'Don't—move,' he said between his teeth as she cradled him in her hips.

Obeying, she held her breath as his body withdrew smoothly, held under a control so savage it transformed his face into a mask of blind desire. Very slowly he eased himself back, then forward again, rocking gently, easily. It was the most wonderful torture. Excitement began to build inside her, each new pleasure stronger and slightly different from the last, growing in subtle, honeyed increments until she could bear it no longer and had to cry out as the rapture took over, cutting her loose, hurling her out over the edge of infinity.

Her body arced, and he, too, cried out, catching the last of her aching sigh in his mouth as he drove into her. She felt him tighten, heard the harsh dragging of his breath, and as he reached the limits of his endurance she cried out again. Rings of sensation expanded through her, exploded into an incandescence so overwhelming that afterwards she wondered whether she had lost consciousness for a few seconds, then receded imperceptibly until she was lying lax and warm and sleepy beneath him.

He should be too heavy, she thought. But surprisingly enough he wasn't. His weight was comforting. It was almost as though she was made to cope with it.

With a quick twist that took her by surprise, he rolled over on to his back. Cool air pulled the tiny hairs over

Mike's body erect. Grabbing for the sheet, she managed to haul a bit of it up her body, but Guy was lying on it, preventing it from coming any further.

She sneaked a wary glance at him, the rapturous certainty of their joining fading. He had his arm over his eyes, as though he was warding off the light from eyes too accustomed to darkness to be able to deal with it. It was an oddly endearing gesture, but Mike looked away quickly. Another kind of chill was creeping through her.

Then he said flatly, 'You don't need to worry about your friends. If you can make love to me like that, from now on they've got security for life.'

Pain was cold and hard in her breast, in her throat, stopping her from replying. The warm lassitude fled as though it had never existed. She said painfully, 'Do you think that's why I—why we——?'

'"Made love" is the expression you want,' he said without inflexion. 'Isn't it? Why else would you make love to me, Mike? After all, we hardly know each other.'

He was killing her, but what could she reply? That she had surrendered because she was in love with him?

Careful not to touch him, she slid off the bed.

'Where are you going?'

She whispered, because there was no expression to be heard in a whisper, no shock, no pain, no grief. 'I want to go back to the hotel.'

'I'll take you.'

'No.'

But he did.

As he left her he said mockingly, 'I hope you enjoyed your stay in the big city, Mike. If you ever decide to move down here——'

She couldn't bear it. She said stonily, 'I doubt if that will ever happen.'

'No.' His teeth showed in the darkness as he smiled. 'What would you do if I asked, Mike?'

'Tell you to go to hell,' she said, averting her face. 'I don't like cities.'

'You're too much a country girl.'

He meant unsophisticated and gauche and naïve and rustic. And easily conned, stupid.

'Yes,' she said, and walked through the door and closed it behind her.

She arrived back home on the overnight bus at eight in the morning; a taxi had taken her to the station only half an hour after she had shut the door on him.

That evening Harry told the staff that there were negotiations with the new owners about redundancy payments. Mike stayed on at the hotel, working herself into exhaustion, until the negotiations were over. Then she packed everything that belonged to her and had them shipped over to Russell to be stored in the garage of an old friend of her mother's.

A week later Harry shot himself. Mike saw to the burial of his ashes beside Dodo's, then drew enough money from the bank to get her to Hamilton, as far away from Guy as she could afford to go. There she stayed in a hostel for women while she searched for a job. She had been working for three months when she saw in the newspaper a photograph of Guy and a very beautiful woman, with a notice of their engagement.

CHAPTER SIX

SEVEN years hadn't made much difference to Russell. Mike was the one who had changed, beyond all recognition if the blank stares she got when she smiled at familiar faces were any indication.

For her the last seven years had been busy, rewarding ones. No doubt that was why they had gone so fast, apart from the first twelve months. A broken heart did that to time, expanded it into empty aeons of bleak misery.

Still, she had overcome her grief, just as she had overcome the disadvantages of being born and brought up in the sticks.

Mike ran a hand through curls that had been artfully tamed and cut into a sophisticated cap for her face. Seven years! A lifetime.

A sardonic little smile curved her mouth. Guy certainly wouldn't find her as naïve as she had been that long ago summer. Those seven years, allied to a striving need to prove herself, had polished and honed her into worldliness.

Finding a career had been hard work, but she had enjoyed it. Her mother had used to tell her that when one door closed another opened. Mike always thought the proverb indicated a state of mind, a willingness to grow and mature, but sometimes it seemed to be almost literally true.

Certainly it had happened for her.

But that was in her other life, the real life that waited for her when she went back to Auckland. For the next three weeks she was going to be in the Bay of Islands. It was the first time she had been back. For years she had tried not to think about the place she had grown up

121

in, until eventually she had realised that by blocking off so much of her life she was giving it immense importance.

Once she understood that, she also understood that her refusal to deal with her past explained why she had never fallen in love again, never found a man who had influenced her as Guy had done. She made friends easily, but when any man tried to step past the invisible border between friendship and attraction she retreated behind barricades so high they were still unbreached.

She had been happy these last years, but always at the back of her mind had been the knowledge that part of her life was unresolved. So she had come back to finish it off, to close the door on the past.

This holiday was to be an exorcism.

Although whether she would have plucked up the courage to return if the land agent hadn't tracked her down with an offer for the section, she didn't know. Just as she didn't know whether she was going to sell the land. It was her last link with her grandparents and her mother.

In fact, she had taken the opportunity to come up a week earlier so that she had more time to consider her actions.

Closing the door of her unit behind her, Mike took a deep breath, inhaling the unforgettable scents of sea and manuka scrub and flowers, seasoned with a faint tang of sunscreen lotion. Her spirits soared; she hadn't realised just how much she missed it all, how large a piece of her soul was still here. After Harry had killed himself she had fled the Bay as though it were poisonous, but deep in her heart she had carried it like a hidden jewel.

Smiling, she walked slowly along the narrow street, enjoying the holiday-makers who laughed and called out and ate ice-creams as they strolled past the waterfront, reluctantly giving way to the occasional car. Swimmers, mostly shrieking children and athletic teenagers exhibiting their skills in front of giggling, scantily clad girls, provided just as intriguing a passing parade as those on shore.

During the last seven years the police station, anachronistically Gothic in inspiration, had been given another coat of pristine white paint, and the Moreton Bay fig tree planted by the first customs officer at Russell over a century before might have gained another half-inch in its massive girth, but those seemed the only differences. Still the same were the painted wooden houses set amid gardens where vivid hibiscuses, brilliant marigolds and lilies and creepers, the strong statements of banana palms and native New Zealand flax all fought for dominance. So was the atmosphere, that of a sleepy little town startled anew each year by its influx of tourists.

Mike turned on to the wharf, inspecting the array of yachts and cruisers in the bay. On one, a particularly large, luxurious cruiser, a man stood with his back to the passers-by, looking out across the bay.

Tall—about six feet—and broad-shouldered, he was clad only in a pair of shorts that emphasised the superb muscle development in his back and thighs. Hair the darkness of the devil's soul was sleeked across a head held high with the devil's self-possession. The sun threw a wash of gold over long, tanned muscular legs and narrow hips, wide shoulders, and arms that revealed an extensive acquaintance with manual labour.

Or a gym, Mike thought, reflexively wary because something deep inside her fluttered into forbidden life. The man could be a model. He certainly looked like something from a glossy magazine or a television studio. That superlative physical presence, combined with the magnificent plutocrat's toy he was standing on, added up to something rich and rare, something more than a little out of place in Russell.

Definitely a figment from some super-heated female fantasy! Behind dark glasses Mike's large eyes scrutinised the man who stood there so arrogantly sure of himself. The odd little niggle of sensation pulled sharply at the pit of her stomach.

A slow feminine voice from behind her breathed, 'Oh, lord, he's *gorgeous*. From the back, anyway. But we can't give him a ten until we've all of him. To get top marks he has to have Apollo's face as well as his body. And there has to be that extra something, too.'

As though he had heard, the man turned his head.

The sun whirled hideously, and Mike closed her eyes, stifling a moan.

Something strange and completely untoward happened to her spine. It melted. And so, she discovered to her horror, did her mind, deliquescing into a sensual, hothouse languor. For a second she almost believed she had been subjected to some kind of psychic assault, but the alarming sensations that rioted through her were more physical than spiritual.

Guy!

So powerful was that shattering moment of recognition that the words of the two women behind her almost didn't register.

'Oh, good grief,' the first one groaned. 'He's got it. That drop-dead masculinity. Look at it, will you? Aloof and beautiful, as detached as a god come slumming to earth. He has to be ten out of ten!'

He couldn't possibly hear them—he was too far away, and there was enough noise from other people on the wharf to drown out that heartfelt assessment—but Mike was sure she saw contempt darken the blue sheen of his eyes. One of the women hastily stifled a giggle as that cold, unsparing gaze came to rest on her.

Never one to back down from a challenge, Mike nevertheless found herself stepping swiftly aside so that the two taller women hid her from Guy's acute eyes.

'God,' the woman in front of her muttered, 'if looks could kill we'd be dead meat. Do you think he heard us?'

The two women sighed in unison as Guy bent to retrieve a towel before going down into the cabin, where, no doubt, his wife waited for him. The smooth, powerful flexion of muscles beneath the gleaming skin made Mike swallow harshly. At least he hadn't recognised her.

It had to be her heightened senses that made her fancy she felt the shock force of that blade-sharp blue gaze focusing between her shoulders all the way down the wharf. He had gone below, so he certainly wasn't watching her. But what on earth was he doing in Russell?

Fate, clearly, was enjoying a little malicious fun at her expense. Panic clutched her stomach, and nausea tasted foul in her mouth. Why, oh, why had she decided to come up a week earlier? When the owner of the units had rung to say there'd been a cancellation, would she like the unit for an extra week, why hadn't she said no?

The moral had to be, she thought, weaving through the crowd on the wharf, do not change your holiday arrangements!

As she beat her retreat Mike made a deliberate effort to compose her mind, but in the shade of the last pohutukawa tree, almost hidden by its wide trunk, she turned to gaze back, her eyes lingering compulsively on the showy cruiser.

Purely physical, she scoffed. Been there, done that. For a moment her pale eyes clouded, became turbid and bleak as old memories drained the colour and life from the day.

She had endured the first year away from the Bay in a kind of yearning terror, torn by fear that she might see him, racked by an impossible hope that one day he would find her, tell her that it had all been a mistake and that he was no longer engaged, that he loved her, would she forgive him...?

Inevitably, her forlorn hope had died, and she had put the past firmly behind her and got on with her life. The passing years had convinced her that she had overcome her vulnerability, until those moments on the wharf had revealed just how wrong she was.

What the hell was he doing here?

And what would she do if she met him—as she easily could?

Her fingers shook as she pushed open the gate to her unit; she blinked to banish the sudden shaming tears that ached behind her eyes. With a relief that was completely out of proportion, she went inside the cool flat, closing the door behind her.

Her watch indicated that it was past lunchtime, but any appetite she might have possessed was gone now, banished by the sight of Guy Lorimer. Her small square chin lifted. Shocked or not, she was going to eat. She was not going to let him rob her of appetite ever again. But once safely in the kitchen she opened the fridge door to gaze with singular distaste at the few edibles inside.

For some reason it grated to remember the awed fascination of the two women who had rated him so highly. Slicing sharply into an avocado, Mike winced as the knife slid across the stone. A swift twist of her wrist had the fruit in half, another flicked the stone on to the bench.

He had looked bigger. Not taller, certainly not more bulky—he was still as lean and vibrantly graceful as he had been seven years ago—but he seemed to take up more space. Blast the man, Mike thought savagely, reaching for a tomato; why wasn't he over on Far Winds, where he belonged, instead of cluttering up Kororareka Bay in his pretentious cruiser?

Seven years ago he had been an extraordinarily handsome man, and he still was, but now his good looks were overshadowed by a hard, uncompromising authority that had blazed across the distance to thoroughly intimidate the two women who had been ogling him.

Forget about him, Mike commanded her reluctant brain. He's the past.

With her chin firmly angled she set the table out on the veranda overlooking the garden, partly shielded from the heat of the sun by the glossy green leaves and white flowers of summer jasmine. Their sweet, evocative scent tugged at her memory, slipping smoothly down the years.

What evil coincidence had prompted her to come up when Guy was here too?

'Stop it!' she said out loud. 'Just stop it, you fool!'

As she took the first bite of salad someone knocked on the door. Although no one from the street could see her, Mike froze like a possum caught in a hunter's spotlight. A wholly unnecessary panic made her want to cower away, safe from prying eyes.

He had recognised her. He must have watched her all the way down the road, noting the unit she went into. Being Guy, he wouldn't go away until he got what he'd come for. Exercising a superhuman effort, she stood up, her features composed into a mask of polite uninterest, went through the little holiday flat, and opened the door.

Dressed in cotton trousers and a fine cotton shirt with its sleeves rolled up to his elbows, Guy said nothing at first, just looked at her with eyes that were the superheated blue of a flame.

Yes, seven years had made a big difference to Guy Lorimer. He wore his handsome face and potent masculinity with a cool command that made him compelling and formidable, totally impressive.

Mike hoped that seven years had made as much difference to her. 'Guy?' she said with calm dispassion, schooling her expression into politeness.

'You saw me on the wharf,' he said crisply.

She nodded. 'Yes. How are you?'

His brows lifted. An undertone of mockery hardened his voice. 'I'm fine. How are you?'

Mundane words, but the emotions that burned beneath them were far from mundane.

'As you see,' she said, rather proud of her dismissive little smile, 'I'm very well.'

His gaze ran over her, slow, thorough, containing more than a hint of insolence. 'The butterfly has well and truly emerged,' he observed. 'Where have you been these years, Mike? Are you married?'

He had no right to ask questions, no right to look at her with that touch of possessiveness, but she would only put herself at a disadvantage if she reacted. 'No,' she said. 'Is your wife with you?'

His glance didn't waver. 'She and I were divorced several years ago.'

'I'm sorry.'

He showed strong white teeth in a smile without humour. 'Are you? Aren't you going to ask me in?'

'No.'

She left it at that. A straight, unadorned negative was always the simplest way to refuse.

He grinned, and something of the younger man who had haunted her dreams, arrogant in the power of his youth and his sexuality, blazed forth for a moment. 'Then come and have a drink with me,' he said, and before she could refuse that too he went on blandly, 'I could always drag you to the pub, or pick you up and carry you, if you refuse.' His fingers looped her wrist, not tightly, but with enough strength to show that he meant what he said.

Mike understood the threat and acquiesced with as good a grace as she could. 'This once,' she said evenly. Her eyes fell to his fingers, bronze against the pale olive of her thin wrist.

'Seven years has made quite a difference,' he said as he reached over and pulled the door to behind her. Audaciously he tucked her hand into the crook of his arm. 'I like it.'

'I'm so glad.' Her voice was sugar-sweet.

He laughed, blue eyes glinting. 'Where have you been these last years, Mike?'

'In Hamilton, then Auckland.' If he had to work to extract every bit of information from her he might give up. How dared he come back and expect her to treat him as though nothing had happened? Even after all this time it hurt to have her unimportance in his scheme of things so heavily underlined.

'Why settle there?'

She shrugged. 'Why not?'

His smile was a brief flash of irony. 'Why not, indeed. Do you often come up here?'

'No.'

The Duke of Marlborough was almost full, the terraces out in the front filled with cheerful, laughing holiday-makers trying to cool off. Nevertheless, that formidable, inherent authority of Guy's got them a table far enough from the road to be somewhat secluded.

'You look,' he said, as the waiter went off with the order, 'very little older, you know. Still the same nymph. More confident, perhaps, but that intriguing air of wildness isn't very far below the surface.'

Her brows rose. Ignoring the caressing note in his voice, she said crisply, 'Pull the other leg, Guy.'

He lifted her arm and kissed her wrist, letting his mouth linger on the smooth skin, his eyes narrowed and amused as they surveyed her suddenly hot face. A quick, thundering pulse swept through Mike's body. Scarlet-faced, she tried to jerk her hand away, but he refused to let her go.

'What the hell do you think you're doing?' Although she tried to make her voice acid and controlled, a ragged note betrayed the headlong flurry of her emotions.

He kissed the palm of her hand and put it on the table, but kept his over it, so that she still couldn't snatch it away.

'That sounds more like you,' he said, his eyes coldly satisfied as they scanned her flushed, furious features. 'It won't work, Mike. I'll just keep asking questions until you've told me all I want to know, so you might as well climb down off that high horse and behave like a normal human being.'

'Why are you here?'

Indolent mockery gleamed in his eyes as they rested on her indignant face. 'I'm on holiday at the moment, but tomorrow I start a round of talks at Far Winds with the chief executives of our various branches.'

'I see.' She had regained her poise now, and with it a little intelligence. Her reaction had been far too extreme. If she wanted to convince him she no longer felt anything for him, she was going to have to behave normally. Her attempt to freeze him off might well have aroused the hunter in him.

After all, ex-lovers, if that was what they were, met all the time without turning a hair. Sophistication was the way to go, not dumb resistance.

Composure, she told herself firmly, composure and a worldly approach; that's what's needed now.

'Tell me what you've been doing these last years,' he invited when the waiter had gone away.

Mike sipped the freshly pressed orange juice before answering serenely, 'Oh, working, learning how to run a business. What about you?'

'I've been based in America and Hong Kong,' he said without emphasis. 'What sort of business?'

'A computer shop. I discovered I enjoyed working with them and selling them.'

'Really. Are you a saleswoman?'

Her voice was cool and level. 'I own my own business. I suppose you could call me a broker or a consultant. I listen to what people really want, as opposed to what they think they want, and then I work out the system that suits them best.'

'Do you deal with businesses too?'

'Yes. I started off with personal computers, but satisfied customers asked me to find them the right system for their businesses, so I've sort of infiltrated the commercial world by the side-door.'

He nodded, his eyes never leaving her face. 'I thought you'd be married by now, with a couple of children.'

Mike hoped that her smile looked entirely natural. 'Not yet,' she said lightly.

Once more that heated blue gaze scanned her face, lingering on her eyes, the cut-off chin, the full, lush mouth. Mike knew she was much more mature than she had been the last time she had seen him, but with this man she felt as though she were stuck in a time warp. Irritated by the heat that crept through her skin, she asked briskly, 'And you? Do you have children?'

'No.'

His voice didn't alter, nor did that steady, somewhat inimical regard, but Mike's sensitised nerves reacted as though he had sworn at her.

'You've grown into yourself,' he said. 'You were a pretty girl, but you're a stunning woman, as I'm sure you know. Those pale eyes hold secrets now, and your mouth is no longer so startlingly alien in an innocent face.'

'*Alien*?' Her brows shot up. She drawled, 'I didn't realise you were so imaginative, Guy.'

His smile was deliberately reminiscent. 'Of course you didn't know, you were such a baby, but that lush mouth damned near drove me mad. I had to keep reminding myself that although you appeared to be a consummate little flirt you were a genuine innocent. Sometimes I even thought that you knew what you were doing to me and were enjoying it.'

Mike stared at him with baffled indignation. 'What do you mean, I was a consummate flirt?'

'You were always flashing your lashes at some damned boy or another.'

Her face felt stiff, but she managed to produce a crooked smile. 'It was all purely professional, I can assure you. God, when I think how naïve I was, I could almost cry. And you thought I was a tease?'

'I was intrigued by you right from the start,' he said idly. 'You were such a puzzling mixture, competent and reserved, almost shy, yet you watched me out of the corner of your eyes as though I fascinated you just as much as you did me. And when I kissed you, you went up in flames, you held nothing back, yet you seemed completely inexperienced. I wondered whether you weren't just a damned good actor.'

Mike took a deep, somewhat impeded breath. She didn't want to talk over old times with him, especially not when he was watching her mouth with the intent, purposeful stare of a hunter.

'As you were,' she said with dulcet, unmistakable emphasis. 'Or didn't it occur to you that you were playing a double game yourself, flirting with me when you had a girlfriend tucked away in the background?'

He said curtly, 'Yes, it occurred to me, often and uncomfortably. It was one of the reasons I was so brutal to you. Guilt brings out the worst in me.'

The orange juice had lost its appeal, but she drained the glass, letting her eyes roam around the laughing, talking crowd. So he'd felt guilty. For some reason this infuriated her.

Along with Russell, she thought caustically, some other things hadn't changed. Once more they were being watched by at least half of the people within sight.

Mike was accustomed to being noticed; her short black hair and pale, translucent eyes were distinctive and unusual enough to attract attention. But it was only when she was with Guy that she was the focus of everyone's interest. Mike hated the sensation of being completely exposed.

According to their natures women watched him openly or covertly; men, too, assessed him with envy and the faint, masculine antagonism that was a sign of respect.

Head held high, she braved it out, wondering how on earth people who earned their living in the public eye coped with such open scrutiny. It put her self-possession to a severe test.

'How long are you here?' she asked, making no attempt to hide the banality of the question.

His expression didn't alter, but she got the impression that he was choosing his words carefully, although when he spoke it was without any noticeable hesitation. 'A week. A fairly high-powered week. You probably don't know, but my grandfather has retired.'

'So you're in charge.'

He showed his teeth in a smile that had no humour in it at all. For a heart-stopping moment he looked like a hunter who had killed. 'Yes. I had to fight for it, but I got there.'

'Did your board think you too young?'

'The company's privately owned; there isn't a board. No, my grandfather had to be convinced. Believe me, he was more difficult than any board could have been.'

Mike's eyes widened deliberately. 'Really? I somehow got the idea that he doted on you.'

'Not my grandfather. He's not into doting.' He swallowed some of his beer, the muscles working in his strong neck. 'Demands are more his line,' he said offhandedly.

'And were the rewards worth the obedience?'

He shrugged. 'At the time I thought they were. I was young and arrogant and single-minded.'

Mike wasn't going to touch that. Keeping her eyes on her hands, she asked lightly, 'Is the gin-palace tied up at the wharf yours?'

He shrugged. 'No, it belongs to—friends who brought me up from Auckland. Why are you here?'

'Just for a holiday.' Her tone was as nonchalant as she could make it. 'Someone wants to buy the section. I thought I'd better come up and see whether I wanted to keep it.'

He watched a slender, blonde woman dressed in the latest and most up-market resort gear sway past, then asked absently, 'How long do you intend to stay?'

Fighting an ignoble pang of jealousy, Mike resisted the temptation to snap. 'Three weeks. It was going to be a fortnight, but the woman who owns the units rang a couple of days ago and said she'd had a cancellation, so I took it.'

He nodded, transferring his gaze back to her face. 'Have you seen anyone from the hotel staff yet?'

'No,' she said shortly. 'I didn't keep in touch. I suppose I should thank you for seeing to it that they got some sort of redundancy.'

His mouth curled into a taunting, unkind smile. 'Don't you remember?' he said. 'We made a bargain. You slept with me and I made sure they didn't go away empty-handed. They were all very grateful. You were the only one who turned the money down.'

Hot colour scorched along Mike's cheekbones. Although she managed to control the involuntary gasp his crudity evoked, she couldn't stop the disdainful words that tumbled from her mouth. 'I hope,' she said distantly, 'that it was worth it.'

'Oh, I've got no complaints. The night we spent together still shines in my memory.' His tone was mordant, rough-edged. 'Your sacrifice was not in vain.'

This time she couldn't keep her eyes from straying defiantly towards his face. But she saw no mockery in his expression. For a single scorching moment his gaze rested on the slight movement of her breasts as she shrugged.

Like an animal in mortal danger, Mike froze. Although Guy's face revealed nothing of his thoughts, his angular features were chiselled into sharp relief, and beneath those disarmingly thick lashes the steel-blue eyes glittered like stars in a metallic summer sky.

Mike saw lust in his expression, and she was terrified, because everything in her leapt to meet it with a wild surge of need. Stormy, uncontrollable sensations flared deep within her in a place she couldn't reach, couldn't regulate, a place where such dark, frightening desire was the norm rather than the exception.

She was shaken by piercing anticipation, followed immediately by a humiliation that ate into the shining edifice of her poise. Apart from that one searing look,

Guy's impressive and altogether admirable restraint had fettered his emotions. Mike hoped fervently that she was able to do the same, although quick colour heated her cheeks and an unexpected tenderness tingled through her lips.

No! Summoning the self-discipline she had worked so hard to attain, she fought a fierce battle for supremacy with responses she had thought dead these last seven years, coercing herself to ignore the nerves that throbbed in an ancient, threatening counterpoint to the cold, hard logic of her brain.

'I'm glad,' she said in her most brisk manner, only to flush as the realisation of what she had said hit her. Hastily she added, 'That things worked out well.'

Irony gleamed in his eyes, but he didn't take her up on her slip. 'Would you like to see Far Winds?' he asked. 'I'm going out there now; I could take you.'

His voice was even and dispassionate, so at variance with that sudden hungry look that Mike began to wonder whether she'd let her imagination run dangerously away with her common sense. She was beginning to realise that where Guy Lorimer was concerned she had forgotten nothing, learned nothing in the past seven years; she was still far too vulnerable to his particular brand of forceful charm.

She shook her head. 'No, thank you.'

'Why?'

'I just don't think it would be sensible,' she countered with grim resolution.

Of course he didn't let her get away with that. 'Why?'

'I don't want to go out to the island with you,' she stated without emphasis.

Winged black brows lifted in an otherwise impassive countenance. 'Scared, Mike?'

Mike finished her drink. She got to her feet, saying quietly, 'Enjoy your holiday, Guy. Goodbye.'

'I'll see you round.'

She thought she felt his eyes on her all the way home, which was ridiculous. Even as she stopped to talk to someone who did recognise her, a woman who used to work as the doctor's receptionist, her skin prickled in involuntary reaction to a man who was well out of sight.

She spent the afternoon lying on a lounger under the jasmine pergola, trying to rest. Unfortunately her brain came back time and again to the sudden, shocking ease with which her body had surrendered to the mysterious, primitive dominion that Guy held over it.

She was not going through that again. Even now, recalling the grey days of misery after she had left Far Winds made her shiver. It was a hard truth to face, that she still wanted him as much as she had ever done. However, she could cope with that. What iced her blood in the lazy heat of the afternoon was that he wanted her, too. She had become adept at reading the signs, and there was no doubt.

'No,' she said out loud, turning over on to her back. A bee buzzed ponderously past, heavily laden with pollen, gleaming gold with some flower's bounty.

Physical attraction was more potent than champagne, but ultimately as ephemeral. As soon as any distance was put between the desirer and the object of that desire, the desire died.

The unfortunate thing about it was that, given the same situation, the attraction returned with unabated strength. She was still vulnerable, which meant that she should cut her holiday short and get back to Auckland, and safety.

For a moment she seriously considered leaving, but Mike had grown up since the day she had fled Far Winds. Running away solved nothing, for Guy was not her problem; his effect on her was. Unfortunately, by some whim of fate and chemistry, she was addicted to him. That had to be why she hadn't found another man to love. Some unintentional, primal quality about him appealed to an elemental need in her. Physically, they were perfectly matched.

Over the years Mike had listened to enough confidences to know that few women had had such a magnificent introduction to making love as she. Guy had been all that every virgin hoped for, tempering his virile male passion with tenderness, intuitively understanding how to please and arouse a woman. He had used his masculinity and his inborn gift of sexuality to short-circuit her inhibitions and summon a pagan, carnal response.

Perhaps that was why she was so hung up on the wretched man, she thought, turning on to her stomach. Her body ached as if she had a fever, making her restless and jittery, unable to enjoy the peace or the warm northern sun.

What was she going to do if he pursued her?

Keep saying no; it was the only safe response. He'd give up sooner or later. Probably sooner. He wasn't in love with her, and there were other women who would be more than happy to give him what he needed.

It was not the bravest decision she had made, but it eased some of the tension in her. Will-power was all she needed, and the sharp, keen memory of how she had felt that dreary, interminable year when she had tried to pick up the pieces of her life again.

Smoothing the frown from between her fine black brows, she picked up the book she had been trying to read for six weeks, and applied herself to it once more.

That evening the telephone rang just as the sun went down. With caution Mike picked it up. A feminine voice said, 'Mike? It *is* Mike Christopher, isn't it?'

Mike's frown eased into recognition and pleasure. 'Nola? Is that you?'

'Yes, of course it is! Oh, Mike, it's lovely to hear you! Marie Renwick rang just a few minutes ago and said she'd been talking to you. Why don't you come out to see us tomorrow?'

'I'd love to,' Mike said, laughing, her spirits rising with miraculous speed. 'Where are you?'

'Out at Far Winds, of course.'

Mike's mouth dropped. She asked faintly, 'What are you doing there?'

'Oh, I bake for the coffee-shop and make the pastries for the restaurant, and back up the chefs and the kitchen staff. Sean's the odd-job man. We've been here ever since the new hotel opened.'

Mike propped her whirling head on her hand. 'So things have worked out well for you,' she said after a moment.

'Couldn't be better. We managed to get—no, I'll tell you all about it when you come out. How about to-morrow? Oh, I'm dying to see you, Mike.'

Guy had said he was visiting Far Winds. But he wasn't likely to be on the ferry out, or even to be wandering around the hotel. No doubt he'd be in conclave with his executives, far from the eyes of any guests.

And Mike really wanted to see what Bishops had done on the island.

'OK,' she said. 'How do I get out?'

'Oh, catch the ferry. We're on the route now, with an hourly service.'

Seven years had certainly altered the island, although the Bay was as full of boats as it had used to be over those long past summers.

As she stepped off on to the wharf Mike couldn't prevent a silent exclamation. Gone were the run-down buildings, the cheerful, unconcerned air of shabby decay. Everything, including the old wharf, had been bulldozed away and replaced by a resort of unashamed modernity.

It had been done very skilfully. From the sea it was almost impossible to discern the buildings that nestled in the curve between the hills and the long sweep of land beside the lagoons. Their stained wooden walls and dark roofs were the exact colour of the leaves on the pohutukawa trees Harry had nurtured, and blended almost imperceptibly into the landscape.

Suspiciously, Mike counted each one of those trees, sighing a little when she realised only one had gone. Even the golf course had been so skilfully fitted into the landscape that it didn't obtrude on the eye.

Nola was waiting for her on the wharf, a little more plump, considerably more grey, her cheerful face lit up with the enthusiasm that Mike remembered so well.

'Oh, Mike!' she exclaimed, hugging her fervently. 'It's great to see you again! I've often wondered how you were getting on, but I can see that you've done well! You look stunning, very smart and posh! Come on, come and see where we live, and I'll make a cup of tea.'

Nola and Sean lived in a house, one of a duplex on the site of the cottage that had been Mike's.

'This is lovely,' Mike said, looking around her at the gardens and the pines. Her heart clenched. The garden had changed very little; mingled with the balsam of the pines was the sweet, old-fashioned scent of the roses her mother had planted, still growing on the trellis, still carefully tended.

'Isn't it just?' Nola beamed proudly around. 'You know, when Bishops bought Far Winds I thought the end of the world had come, but really, it was the best thing that could have happened to us. We have a lovely life now.'

Her words hit Mike on the raw. Things had worked out well for Nola and Sean, but Harry had killed himself rather than face life without Far Winds. She said hastily, 'I'm so glad. The hotel certainly looks as though it's flourishing.'

'Flourishing! Oh, it's certainly "flourishing". It's just won an airline award for the best hotel in the North Island, and the manager, Ron Sellers, says he's not going to be content until we're the best one in the South Pacific!'

While Nola made a pot of tea she expanded on her theme. Clearly she was very happy with her life.

When the cup of tea was steaming in front of Mike, and after she had dithered happily over a plate of delicious cakes before choosing one, Nola commanded, 'Now, tell me what you've been doing since we saw you last. What did you do when you left Far Winds?'

'I went to Hamilton.'

'Why Hamilton?'

'I just liked the sound of it,' Mike said vaguely. 'I applied for every vacant situation in the newspaper for a fortnight and then I got a job as receptionist for a firm that sold computers.'

'You always were interested in computers. You used to try to coax Harry into buying one, remember? You went around all the shops and worked out a system that would save both time and mistakes.'

Yes, Mike remembered. 'And Harry said he was too old to bother about them. I learned a lot in my first job. Because it was a smallish firm they let me have a go at everything I wanted to do. But after a year I'd exhausted the possibilities there, so I moved to Auckland and found a job in a similar place, but bigger.'

Even now she refused to admit that it was another notice in the newspaper, to the effect that Guy Lorimer had gone to take over Bishops' Asian operations from Hong Kong, that had decided her to move. She gave a lop-sided smile. 'I found out later that I actually got the job because I reminded the owners of their daughter, who'd just got married in Western Australia! The owners believed that women are better at selling than men because they listen, instead of trying to sell everyone the latest thing off the factory floor whether they need it or not.'

'I'm inclined to agree,' Nola said emphatically. 'So you sell computers for a living?'

'Actually, I own the business now. When the Carters decided they wanted to live near their daughter and the grandkids a couple of years ago, they sold me the firm. So now I make a living matching people and firms with the perfect set-up for their needs.'

'And do you really like it? It sounds awfully dry.'

'I do enjoy it. Although I have to do more organisation and business now, rather than the selling, which is what I really like.'

Mike smiled a little ironically at Nola's awed expression. They drank tea and gossiped about the others who had worked at Far Winds—Nola seemed to act as a kind of relay station for information—and then Mike said diffidently, 'If you don't mind, I'd like to go up to Harry's and Dodo's grave. I brought some flowers to put on them.'

'I wondered who the others were for.' Nola looked appreciatively at the lilies Mike had given her. 'Of course I don't mind! In fact, I have to go across to the kitchen now for an hour or so, so you just wander round. You'll see a lot of changes.'

Mike did. The island had been transformed, the golf course carefully designed to make the most of its scenic beauty. In spite of the heat, the fairways and greens were being used to the utmost.

One of the world's leading professionals had designed the course, and an equally brilliant landscape artist had designed a setting worthy of it. Groves of trees, mostly indigenous, had been chosen for their flower or form.

They were beautiful, but it was the native bush in the gullies, so much higher than it had been seven years ago, that caught Mike's attention. Tree-ferns, bright green Catherine wheels against the darker, more sombre tones of the bush, were reaching towards the sky in their hundreds, as were nikau palms. Seedling kauri trees, still spindly, a far cry from the monolithic trees they would eventually be after several hundred years, poked their fresh green needles through the canopy of manuka.

A nature walk wound through the cool, freshly scented bush; at intervals there were notices in several languages, pointing out trees or shrubs of interest. The path seemed to be heading towards the hilltop where Harry and Dodo lay, so Mike followed it, puffing slightly up the last, steep pinch.

A block of granite marked their resting place. Seats were placed near by to take advantage of the view, and a mosaic map of the Bay of Islands gave those with a passion for information something to discover.

The grave was tidy and neatly kept. Earlier in the day someone had put a little wreath of hibiscus flowers on the grey stone. They would die in the night, but for now their pure, saturated colours glowed like a miniature sunset against the plain marker. Mike put her bunch of lilies beside them, then fumbled in her bag for a handkerchief.

Guy said from behind, 'I thought it was you I saw trudging up the hill.'

She sniffed, keeping her head lowered.

In an entirely different voice he said, 'They're together now,' and his arms came around her in a wonderfully gentle embrace, holding her against his lean body.

'Dodo was a great friend of my mother's,' she said into his shoulder. 'And Harry let me stay here when Mum died. He was kind.'

'Poor devil.'

She remembered that it was this man who had killed Harry, and pulled away.

'Perhaps,' he said quietly, 'it was the only way out he could cope with. But I don't think I'd have given up so easily. Cancer isn't a death sentence now, and it wasn't then.'

What on earth was he talking about? 'Cancer?' she croaked, staring at the stark angles and lines of his profile, silhouetted against the blazing sea and sky.

'Yes.' Something flickered in the burnished depths of his eyes. 'Didn't you know? He'd been given a year to live three months before. He decided he didn't need it.'

Guy smiled unpleasantly. 'It wasn't losing the hotel that made him kill himself,' he finished.

'He and Mum nursed Dodo,' she said through lips that felt slack and numb. 'She was in such pain...' She couldn't say anything more, but she knew that shame was plain on her face.

'So you've held me responsible for all these years,' he went on, giving no quarter. 'How annoying for you to have to give up such a cherished misconception. Poor Mike!'

Mike blew her nose. 'I'm sorry,' she said numbly.

'Oh, don't be. You know, at first I was convinced he was your father, you were so protective of him, but eventually I realised that you weren't so much protective of him as antagonistic towards me.' He looked out across the Bay, out past the Ninepin Rock and Purerua Peninsula to the hazy blue of the Cavalli Islands to the north. 'And you were so very prickly for exactly the same reason that I did my damned best to keep away from you, and failed. We looked at each other that first time and something happened.'

'I don't believe in love at first sight.' Mike had recovered herself enough to speak scornfully.

He gave a short bark of laughter. 'It wasn't love.'

In spite of her justifications the preceding afternoon some unregenerate part of Mike must have been hopeful, because she felt a pang of pain so acute that she had to hold herself still and rigid for long seconds, until it ebbed. She wanted to tell him to stop it, to go away and leave her to her illusions.

'I know——'

'And it's still there,' he interrupted, 'just as much a threat to both of us as it was seven years ago.'

She couldn't bear to hear him talking in that hard, impervious voice about something from which she had never been able to recover. No other man had ever measured up to Guy. She had gone out with quite a few, but sooner or later she had ended each association, because his image, the memory of his lovemaking, was burned in letters of fire across her psyche. She had almost given up any thoughts of marrying, of having children. Somehow he had managed to stamp his imprint so deeply on her that the thought of making love with any other man made her gorge rise.

And now he was telling her that it wasn't love, that it was nothing but an animal appetite.

Staring blindly out to sea, she said, 'Don't you think you're making too much of an old infatuation?'

'It isn't dead,' he said mercilessly. 'I haven't been able to get you out of my mind. And it's still very much alive for you, too.'

Swiftly, Mike returned, 'That doesn't mean we have to do anything about it.'

'Is that what you want? To spend the rest of your life wondering what might have happened if only we'd been brave enough to grasp the nettle?'

'No,' she said jerkily, stepping back. 'No, damn you; don't touch me.'

But he did. His face carved into purposeful lines, he caught her wrist, holding it so that his thumb settled over the fragile veins. Mike's breath tangled in her throat; she saw nothing but the hard demand in his expression, the explicit ruthlessness of a male who wanted a woman beyond all logic. Her heart sped up unbearably. He was watching her hand curl, the fingers tighten with the effort to keep still. A mocking little smile tugged harshly at the corner of his mouth.

'Listen,' he said, and pulled her hand against his chest, forcing the palm flat over his heart. His eyes held hers fiercely, the darkness at the heart of them expanding until she could see only a thin rim of blue flames.

The thunder of his heartbeat drove into her soft palm, drowning out everything except the shrill sound of the cicadas.

'I want you,' he said softly. 'I've wanted you for seven years. You spoiled my marriage; you burrowed into my brain and my body like a parasite, destroying my pleasure, eating at my self-control. When I saw you walk along the wharf yesterday I had to turn away because my body reacted instantly, violently, to the sight of you. I thought I was bloody well imagining things, that you were an illusion sent to taunt me, but I couldn't control myself, not my body, not my mind or my emotions.'

Mike said harshly, 'I don't want to hear this. I don't want anything to do with you. I despise you.'

He laughed again, a sound that sent chills through her. 'I know,' he said roughly. And then, looking over and above her, 'Oh, bloody hell! Of all——'

She managed to turn her head. A small group of laughing people, Japanese at a guess, emerged from the bush, pretending to huff loudly. Relief, sweet and all-pervading, flooded through her.

CHAPTER SEVEN

'LET'S get out of here,' Guy snapped, unceremoniously urging her down the other side of the hill towards Tuesday Bay, a small cove almost hidden by the dense, silver-backed leaves of the two huge pohutukawa trees that overhung the apricot sand.

'Stop it, Guy! I don't want to go with you,' she said desperately as soon as she got her breath. She dragged her arm free, rubbing the wrist. He hadn't hurt her, but she wasn't above taking advantage of her sex to keep him at a distance.

He stopped and looked down at her. 'Shall I show you and everyone up on the hill just how much you want to go with me?' he suggested evenly.

Mike's whole body went cold. 'No,' she said in a mortified voice.

Two family groups were pottering along the little beach. Casting them a look of loathing, Guy said, 'We can't talk here, and I'm due back for another round of bloody meetings in ten minutes. Have dinner with me tonight.'

'What good will talking do?' she asked wearily.

He looked down at her. The implacable determination in his eyes, on his face, didn't ease, but she thought she saw sympathy and a kind of fellow-feeling there, too. 'Poor Mike,' he said with a twisted smile. 'Does it frighten you? It terrifies me, too.'

She said desolately, 'It's degrading.'

'Wanting each other?' He was watching her with calculating eyes, stripping with his narrowed, fixed gaze the thin layer of poise from the seething turbulence of her emotions.

'It wouldn't be so bad if there was anything more to it than that,' she said, trying to prevent her forbidden excitement from showing in her voice. 'But to gratify sex by itself, with nothing to back it up, *is* degrading.'

His brows lifted. For a long moment they looked at each other, Mike's eyes shadowed by her memories of past pain, Guy's hooded, almost secretive.

When he spoke her heart sank. 'I wasn't lying when I said I'd never forgotten you. That night we made love is still as fresh in my memory as if it were yesterday. You haven't forgotten, either. Your reaction when you saw me was fairly obvious. I think we need a bit of exorcism.'

All remaining hope withered away, so tenuous and frail a yearning that she hadn't even known it existed until it died. He didn't love her, and of course she didn't love him.

Then what was it that still bound them to each other after seven years apart? It was an enchantment, a mocking obsession that ensnared them both in its sinister sorcery. It was stupid to grieve for a love that had never existed; she too had understood that exorcism was the only thing that would break the chains that held them together. But would an affair deliver them from this terrible, consuming passion?

Nothing else has, she thought, then shook her head wildly, horrified at the direction her thoughts were taking. 'No.'

Harshly, Guy said, 'What can we do, then? Go around for the rest of our lives, or until passion dies, whichever comes first, wondering whether, if we'd been braver, less cowardly, we might have found some satisfactory solution to this "degrading" passion?' His voice was pitilessly sarcastic.

Mike bit her lip, approaching a decision so unexpected, so against the logical, reasonable conclusions of yesterday, that for a wild moment she wondered whether he was able to cast spells.

Seven years of her emotional life had been wasted because she couldn't get this man out of her mind, out of her life. She wanted to be free of him, to find a man she could love and marry and have children with, a man who could offer love and tenderness and companionship instead of the blinding flashpoint of desire she shared with Guy.

Even though his coldly pragmatic view chilled her soul, perhaps he was right. Perhaps the only way to overcome her weakness was to indulge in an affair until they were both exhausted and sated, sick of each other, all passion spent and scattered like ashes tossed in the wind.

'All right,' she said abruptly.

His glance held hers, dark and turbulent, almost antagonistic. 'Just like that? You do know what you're agreeing to, don't you?'

'Yes.' Glittery with aggression, her eyes gave no quarter. 'An affair, nothing more.'

'Is that all you want?'

Her smile was hard and contemptuous, mostly of herself. 'That's all that's possible, Guy.'

He picked up her hand and kissed it, his tongue caressing the palm with sensuous impact. Tiny heated runnels of sensation loosened Mike's breath, drained her will-power away. If he'd shown any sign of satisfaction she would have recanted, but there was no smugness in his savage smile.

'I have a suite at the hotel,' he said. 'We'll eat dinner there.' He sensed Mike's precipitate withdrawal, and knew it for what it was. 'What's the problem?' he demanded.

'Nola will guess...'

His brows drew together in a bleak frown. 'I'm not going to sneak around.' His voice was clipped and arrogant. 'Hole-and-corner affairs are not my style.'

'And flaunting the fact that I'm a mistress is not mine,' she flashed.

He asked in a swift, angry undertone, 'How many men's mistress have you been since you slept with me, Mike?'

Danger played like lightning all around her, but she stood her ground. 'You have no right to ask me that. You seduced me when you were engaged to another woman.'

'No,' he said. 'I wasn't engaged to Caroline then.'

Staring stonily over a sea so blue and tender that it wounded her heart, she said, 'You must have been damned close to it. It was only a few weeks later that you announced your engagement. Were you sleeping with her?'

'Yes.'

His curt voice warned her not to continue, but her bitter, resentful anger had no place for prudence or caution. 'Did you ever tell her that you'd slept with me?' she demanded, swinging to face him.

The severe, beautiful lines of his face were disciplined by his remorseless will into a grim, dangerously menacing mask. 'No,' he said evenly. 'I didn't tell her.'

'It meant so little to you,' she taunted, hurting herself with her words like a flagellant. 'Just an easily forgotten roll in the hay with a stupid kid.'

'That was not the reason. I don't lie, Mike. I never forgot you, or the way we made love.'

Mike took a deep breath, retreating into the restraint that had become an integral part of her. Where had that anger come from? It was far too revealing. She said thinly, 'It doesn't matter.'

'I think it does.' Frowning, he glanced at his watch. 'Mike, I do have to get back. We can talk tonight. Are you coming back with me, or do you want to stay here?'

'I'll come back with you.' Halfway along the beach she asked, 'How long is your meeting this afternoon?'

Time spent with Nola would give her a respite from the hell-broth of emotions she had glimpsed beneath her own cool and composed surface. Mike was afraid, because it seemed to her that the calm command of herself that she had been so proud of, had worked so hard to acquire, was nothing but a carefully constructed veneer over another, hitherto latent Mike, one who was more than the child she had been when she had left Far Winds, but a different woman from the one who organised her professional life in Auckland so efficiently.

'I should be free by five.' His frown had deepened and he opened his mouth as though to carry on speaking, but when she looked expectantly at him he closed it firmly.

Mike transferred her gaze straight ahead. 'It seems a pity to have to work in such beautiful surroundings.'

His smile was sardonic. 'Everyone should work in beautiful surroundings. What will you do?'

'I'll talk to Nola.' She hesitated a moment before saying, 'What made you give her a job here?'

'Her cooking. She's brilliant with pastries and cakes. Even the chef agrees that he can't do as well. And Sean is a reasonable odd-job man. He just needs someone to make sure he does his job.'

Guy's voice was dry, as was her answering smile, remembering the night they had spent huddled together on the runabout.

Was that when she had started to lose her heart? No, that had happened when she had looked at him for the first time.

Back at the hotel he said, 'I'll see you later, in the foyer at five.'

Mike nodded again, but her eyes slid away from his dark, compelling gaze.

He said softly, 'Don't change your mind, Mike. I'll come looking for you if you do.'

And before she could give him the spirited answer her pride required, he turned away and left her.

She spent the rest of the afternoon with Nola, talking, catching up with news of the Bay, hiding the maelstrom of her emotions with laughter and reminiscences.

When the children arrived home on the ferry from school, she became reacquainted with them, charming them out of their sudden adolescent bashfulness, and Sean's arrival for afternoon tea was accompanied by a further round of talk.

At last Mike said reluctantly, 'I'd better get going, I suppose.'

'I'll come with you.' Nola looked at her watch as she got to her feet. 'Before you go, write your address and telephone number in my address book. I'm not a great letter writer, but we can at least send each other Christmas cards. Hurry, you'll just catch the ferry as it is.'

'I'm not going home on the ferry,' Mike said, scribbling into the book Nola thrust at her.

Nola lifted her brows. 'How are you getting back, then?'

Mike smiled, trying to sound as casual as she hoped her attitude was. 'Oh, I met Guy up on the hill, and he asked me to have dinner with him.'

Nola's surprise was plain, but she waited until they were out of the house before saying in an elaborately casual manner, 'Guy's nice, isn't he? When he came back a year ago I didn't think he'd recognise me—well, six years is a long time, isn't it?—but he did. He even told me to call him Guy, not Mr Lorimer, which is what everyone else calls him. I thought he'd lost touch with you.'

'He did,' Mike said wryly.

'Oh.' After a moment Nola went on, 'As it happens, he asked me if I knew where you were...' Her voice trailed away. When Mike said nothing she went on, 'I suppose he felt a bit responsible for you. Well, we all did, especially after Harry died. I know I worried about you for quite some time. Did you know his wife? Guy's, I mean.'

'No.' Mike was rather proud of her steady voice and calm demeanor. 'No, until yesterday I hadn't seen Guy for seven years.'

'Oh, I see. So it was just coincidence, you both being here at the same time?'

'Pure coincidence,' Mike replied.

'I wonder what she was like, his wife. We never saw her. They were still living overseas when they separated.'

Nola kept sliding little sideways looks at Mike, clearly unable to make up her mind whether to speak or not. After a moment she ploughed on. 'He's—very attractive, isn't he? And impressive. Women like him. He's probably too popular for his own good.'

'Do you mean he's promiscuous?'

Nola looked shocked. 'No, I don't mean that at all. I just mean that he's *very* attractive. Women make a dead set at him, but he doesn't seem in the least interested. I think his marriage killed something in him. I wouldn't like to see you hurt.'

Mike's smile was bittersweet. 'Don't worry,' she said. 'I'm not going to throw myself at him.'

Nola didn't look convinced, but she said nothing more.

As it happened, Mike walked into the foyer just as Guy was going across to the lift with a group of people who wore their executive status like flags. He was still clad informally in an open-necked shirt and trousers, a far cry from the suits of the others, but there was no mistaking who was boss. They weren't deferential so much as respectful, listening to Guy as he talked incisively, his expression absorbed, that leashed vitality turning his colleagues into colourless ciphers.

A cold patch in the region of Mike's stomach expanded. This man, ruthless, dynamic, the head of a billion-dollar business, was so distant from plain Mike Christopher that they had absolutely nothing in common.

She half turned, ready to walk out again, but he saw her move and those eyes clashed with hers across the tiled floor of the foyer in an order that was none the less imperative for being unspoken.

Mike stood poised for flight, yet unable to move. Guy said something, left the group, and came across to her, his smile not echoed in his eyes. Behind him the group gave her one comprehensive glance, then got into the lift and disappeared.

'Don't run away,' he commanded quietly, touching her cheek in a gesture so possessive that sparks kindled in the pale fire of her gaze.

'You're busy.'

He knew it was an excuse. He said, 'No, I've finished with them. Come on up.'

The suite he took her to was decorated with a spare, informal luxury that appealed immensely to Mike. She told him as much and he said, 'Heavily classical furniture wouldn't have fitted the place. I wanted it to look vaguely tropical, yet be cosy when it gets colder. A lot of our visitors come for the golf in the winter.'

'It's beautiful,' she said simply. 'You've made an excellent job of it.'

'Yes.' He looked around the room. 'Although I must admit that I had little to do with it, beyond setting guidelines. I left for Hong Kong fairly soon after I got married. Would you like a drink? Orange juice?'

She shook her head. 'Something a little stronger, I think.'

He chose champagne, uncorking and pouring it with the skill of long practice. 'I think we should drink to us,' he said softly.

Mike bit her lip. They had drunk the same toast the night they had made love.

She wasn't going to back out now. She didn't know whether she could even if she wanted to; his parting comment hours before had been a definite threat. But apart from that, he had such a powerful effect on her that running away was no longer a viable option. Need for him was a forbidden enchantment, a bitter hunger that had eaten into her soul for the last seven years. She had tried ignoring it, and sublimating it with the demands of her career. Neither had worked. Now she would surrender to it, and, by giving in, rob it of power and strength.

'To us,' she said quietly, and lifted her glass and drank.

He drank at the same time, his eyes fixed on hers, heated and merciless. The colour that suffused her cheekbones proved how precarious her composure was. 'I need to clean up,' she said.

'The bathroom's through there, across the bedroom. Use the wrap hanging on the door if you like.'

The bedroom had an enormous low bed in it, covered in a material glowing with blues and golds that echoed the sunlit sea through the windows. After one quick glance Mike hurried by.

It had been relatively easy to make the decision to sleep with him. It was not going to be so easy to embark on an affair with any degree of sophistication. She had no experience in being a mistress. Or a lover, come to that.

She washed her bra and pants out, switched on the heated towel rail, and hung them along it. The shower was refreshing and she stayed in it longer than normal, using the toiletries she had found in a cupboard, expensive brands that whispered of wealth and a discreet, cosmopolitan world of sensuality. The scent, stimulating yet seductive, clung to her sleek skin and her hair even after she had patted herself dry.

The bra and pants were dry enough to put back on, damp enough to make her grimace. Swiftly she wriggled into them, listening with nerves that were distinctly on edge for any sound from the bedroom. A comb flicked her hair into shape; in ten minutes it would be dry, the curls forming a riotous cap over her face. She applied the lip gloss that was her sole cosmetic, then with a distasteful face pulled on the linen trousers and shirt.

When she came back into the sitting-room he looked up from the desk where he was working, and the blue eyes kindled. With one lithe movement he got to his feet, his smile deepening as he came towards her.

But all he said was, 'Finish your drink. I thought we might have dinner on the balcony.'

The balcony looked out over one of the lagoons. Sipping her wine, Mike appreciated how skilfully the suite was shielded by plants from the rest of the resort. Even noise, no respecter of screens, couldn't break through the thick greenery. They might just as well be on a desert island.

'This is lovely,' she said, hoping that the champagne would desensitise her jumping nerves. 'Of all your hotels, what's your favourite?'

Guy knew what she was doing, of course. His smile was tinged with cynicism, but he answered smoothly, 'I like them all, for different reasons. One of these days you must tell me which one you like most.'

Her glass arrested on its way to her mouth, Mike stared at him, her eyes wide and shocked above the rim.

'I don't intend this to be a one-night stand like last time,' he said deliberately, not taking his eyes from hers. 'You'll travel with me, of course. Why not?' he asked, as she shook her head.

'I've got a living to earn,' she said painfully, lowering the glass. 'I can't get away very often.'

'The devil you can't.' He used the time it took to drain his glass to reimpose control over the swift, blazing flare of anger that had hardened his face. 'OK, let it go; we'll work out the details later. Do you play golf?'

'Not as a sport. Why?'

'We have to start somewhere,' he said ironically. 'Do you realise how little we know about each other? For example, I'll bet you didn't know that I looked you up in the telephone directory the first day I arrived back in Auckland to live.'

'No,' she said faintly.

His smile was lop-sided. 'You weren't there, of course.'

'No, I've got an unlisted number.'

'Have you had trouble?'

She reacted swiftly to the terse enquiry. 'Not obscene calls, nothing like that. It's just that some of my clients wanted to have their source of information on tap all the time. They didn't seem to realise that I needed time to relax away from computers!'

'So that explains why you didn't turn up in any directory in New Zealand.'

She smiled faintly, 'You went through every telephone directory?'

'Someone did.' He poured more champagne. 'I gave everyone on Far Winds strict instructions that if you ever turned up here I was to be told immediately, and that you weren't to be allowed off the island until someone had extracted your address from you.'

Mike's mouth dropped slightly open. 'You've got a damned nerve,' she breathed after an appalled moment, remembering Nola's insistence on getting her address, and the subsequent subtle warning.

He showed his teeth in a humourless smile. 'I let you go once. I don't make the same mistake twice.'

'What would you have done if I'd been married?' she asked indignantly.

'I expected you to be. That time I stayed at Far Winds you seemed to spend most of your time flirting with boys. It was when I admitted that I was jealous of them, of every one of them, that I realised I wanted you to look at me the way you looked at them. However, I didn't want you to flirt with me. I wanted to take you, make you mine in the most basic, primitive way possible.' His voice was raw. 'Only it was obvious that I couldn't do that. You might or might not have been innocent, but you were almost completely unsophisticated, and there was no way I could envisage you fitting into my life. I felt the kind of physical attraction I'd never felt before, but it wasn't love, and it wasn't enough. Not even love is enough. My parents loved each other, but they couldn't live together, and in some way it broke both of them.

I'd already decided what sort of woman I was going to marry, and you were nothing like her.'

'So you behaved like an older brother,' she said acidly, hating him for being so cold-blooded and calculating.

'I tried. And, in spite of some lapses, I managed to stick to it. But then you came down to Auckland. I was delighted, thrilled like a kid who gets the birthday present his parents said he couldn't have. But you were furious, and so was I, too damned soon. You thought I was going to throw all those people off the island and out of work without a penny, and I was having a hell of a time convincing my grandfather that Bishops couldn't do that. The day you arrived filled with righteous indignation, he'd told me that he hadn't raised me to be soft and easy to overawe, that I was a grave disappointment to him, and that perhaps I wasn't the right person to take over Bishops. I was furious, and frustrated. You came at just the wrong time.'

'So you decided to make me suffer.' Not looking at him, she spoke with a hard-won detachment. She didn't think she would ever forgive him for the events of that night seven years ago, but at least she knew now why he had behaved like that.

'*No*. I was very reluctantly accepting that my nicely planned life, with its suitable wife, was going out the window.' His smile was without humour. 'I blamed you, because until I went to Far Winds I'd had my life well under control.'

'Why did you go? Surely it wasn't good business practice? Someone might have recognised you.'

'So my grandfather said, but I was determined. I needed a holiday and I was cocky enough to convince myself that no one would know me.'

'You were right, of course.' She hoped that her voice was impersonal, calm.

'And there you were, maddening and exciting and unforgettable. When I kissed you, you melted like honey in my arms. But even then I was quite arrogantly sure that I wouldn't succumb. So I took you out to dinner, and you wore that white lace thing with little pearl buttons that pleaded to be opened, one after the other...' He stopped, and laughed cynically. 'God, for years I cursed myself for not undoing those pearl buttons! It was just as well I was leaving the next morning, because I didn't intend to sleep with you, and that evening you provoked me almost beyond control.'

'What changed your mind?' It astounded her that she could speak so clearly, so steadily, when her whole self was writhing on a rack of disappointment, of old, remembered anguish superimposed over fresh pain and foreboding.

His smile was twisted. 'My whole life was in turmoil, and you hadn't come down to Auckland to see me; you'd come to help your friends. You made it more than clear that you despised me. It got me on the raw, so I behaved like a bastard.'

'You did, indeed.' Even now, after seven years, she spoke through her teeth.

'Yes. I was going to punish you. But it didn't last; I couldn't keep it up. And then we made love.' He looked down into his glass. 'It was unbearably wonderful, but—when I said you'd done it for your friends, I wanted you to laugh, to tell me you loved me. Even though I knew a marriage between us would be as doomed as my parents' was. You didn't tell me you loved me; you left me, and I let you go. I held out until Harry died. Then I came up to Far Winds to look for you, only to find that you'd left the island, and no one knew where you were.'

Sheer astonishment held her rigid, locked in silence. He was looking into his champagne, his profile a strong statement against the softly coloured sky. The tiny lines fanning out from the corners of his eyes were almost hidden by the thick, long lashes.

Mike asked incredulously, 'You came up to Far Winds to find me?'

He shrugged. 'I thought I might have made you pregnant.'

'And if you had, what were you planning to do about it?' She couldn't hide the sharp note of sarcasm in her voice. 'Pay for an abortion?'

'No.' He looked up at her, his eyes flat and accusing. 'I was going to suggest that you marry me, pregnant or not. You see, I hadn't been able to get you out of my mind, out of my heart. My plans for my life seemed arid and infinitely unattractive. But you were gone, and no one knew where you were. I came back to Auckland, but you'd dropped out of the world. I couldn't find you.'

'So you married Caroline.'

'Yes.' He looked out of the window, his expression cold and ruthless. 'And discovered that, although a marriage where two people love each other but are unsuitable may be hell, even worse is one where the partners are suitable but not in love. Thank God we didn't have children. In the end the divorce was a relief to both of us.'

Some tension she hadn't been conscious of relaxed, soothing away a sore place in her heart. 'So when you saw me at Russell you decided to discover whether you could warm up a few cold embers.'

His smile was ironic, without humour. 'I knew you were at Russell.'

Mike stared at him. 'How did you know?'

'I'd remembered you had a section here. I managed to find your address from the council rolls, and I made an offer for it through the land agent to get you up here.' His smile was oblique. 'And the land agent told me when you were coming, even where you were staying, although you weren't supposed to be here until next week.'

'The unit owner had a cancellation,' Mike said automatically. 'Why? Why did you go to so much trouble? Why did you want me to come up *here*?'

He didn't reply immediately, and when he did he didn't answer her question. 'It seemed appropriate. As for why—well, I thought it was because I always felt guilty.'

'You never made me any promises,' she said directly.

'I should never have slept with you. But I was punished too, because nothing was ever like it again. You marked me for life. So yes, I wanted to see you again, find out whether I'd just been spinning impossible dreams. In fact, I told myself that when I saw you, probably married, the magic would flee and I'd be able to go on with my life.'

'What would you have done if I had been married?'

His smile was sardonic. 'It's immaterial, isn't it? You aren't, and the magic is just as strong as ever. I saw you walk along the road towards the wharf and I was as giddy and excited as a kid in the throes of his first crush. I don't care how many lovers you've had since we made love the first time, Mike; I want to love you now.'

So that you can get me out of your system, she thought wearily. Well, why the hell not? She too had been locked in that time warp of emotion, unable to fall in love, unable to free herself from the primitive spell he had woven about her seven years ago.

Eventually the sexual bewitchment must fade, and she'd see Guy with clear eyes, just as he would her. They'd be able to give each other up gracefully and put the whole episode behind them, behave like mature, sophisticated adults.

Perhaps they might discover that absence had given a spurious edge to an appetite that had faded long since. Even as she found herself hoping that it was so, she knew that it was not. Champagne bubbles fizzed softly on her tongue, slid effervescently down her throat. Whatever was between them had lasted for seven years; it had a power of its own.

She nodded. 'Yes,' she said simply.

He took a step towards her, stopping with a muttered curse as there was a knock on the door. It was the waiter with a trolley.

They ate a superb meal of swordfish steaks and salad on the balcony, drank a little more champagne with it, and watched the sun set riotously, the sky take on a rare green transparency, and then the winking in of the first star.

Perhaps it was the champagne, but instead of the pauses heavy with innuendo that Mike half expected they talked easily of many things, of books they liked and disliked, of places they had been, of how they saw the currently fashionable movements. And this time she was able to keep up with him.

He had a dry, astringent common sense that she enjoyed, as she enjoyed the sensation of sharpening her mind against the cold, incisive intelligence of his.

At last, when the silent waiter had removed the dinner things, Guy said quietly, 'Come to me, Mike.'

She had been fiddling with her half-empty glass, turning the slim flute in her hands, watching the tiny beads of bubbles rise in thin streams to the top of the golden liquid. Without talking, without even looking at him, as if a great weight had rolled from her, she put the glass down and went across to him.

'So docile,' he mocked softly. 'Are you always going to be like this?'

Mike lifted thick lashes, met without flinching the molten blue impact of his gaze. Until then he had been holding himself under rigid control; now she saw that iron restraint begin to break up, shatter into a million shards as he gave in to the need that had been eating at them both for seven long years.

His thumb gently brushed along her mouth. 'Such a lush, wanton mouth,' he murmured, his gaze licking along its full contours like flame. 'When I met you, you looked like a little girl except for that mouth, and the strange intensity of pale, crystalline eyes set between black lashes. I wanted you rather more than I'd wanted any other woman, and I felt like a pervert for desiring innocence so much.'

'I was twenty,' she protested, shocked at the way her lips grew warm and throbbing under his light touch.

'You were a baby, running yourself into the ground trying to do three jobs at once.' He suddenly bent and picked her up, his eyes very bright and steady as she gasped. 'But you're not a baby now. You're a woman, and I want you so much I can feel the need eating into my gut.'

He put her down on the side of the huge bed and knelt to remove her sandals. His hands on her feet were cool and knowing, almost caressing. The heat that had been simmering through Mike's bloodstream began to build, coursing through her veins, taking with it inhibitions and shame and worry.

'Such strong, slender calves,' he said quietly as he ran his hands up her legs. 'Take your clothes off for me, Mike.'

Heat raced across her olive skin, carrying with it a strange, heavy lassitude that slowed her movements, weighted her limbs, gathered in her breasts. Meeting his eyes with no shyness, she slid free the buttons from her shirt, watching the colour gather darkly along his cheekbones, the blue of his eyes turn into a smoky inferno.

Her bra was not in the least seductive, merely cool cotton with a front fastening. Although she couldn't control the fluttering of her lashes she unclipped the clasp with steady fingers. It gave her a strange, sultry feeling to be looked at as though her slow movements were unwrapping all the treasures of Arabia.

She wasn't embarrassed when the little bra fell away, not even when her nipples peaked underneath the heated intensity of his eyes.

'Now it's your turn,' she said hoarsely.

Guy leaned forward and kissed the pink tip of one breast. Fire shot from it to the fork of her body, setting the hidden pathways in her body aflame. Mike took a sharp, impeded breath. At that moment more than anything in the world she wanted him to take the soft aureole in his mouth, but he smiled and got to his feet.

As he took off his shirt she removed the rest of her clothes. Mike knew no seductive movements or gestures so she followed her instincts and watched as he pulled off his shirt and trousers. Again her breath jagged through her lungs. He was magnificent, and although she had known the full sensual force of his body she was still a little alarmed at his proud, jutting masculinity.

'No,' he said, correctly reading her expression as she looked away. 'We'll take it nice and easy, gentle and smooth, and you'll find we fit together perfectly. We did last time, remember?'

Before she had a chance to reply he lifted her and pulled the covers back. The fine lawn sheet was cool on her back, but Mike was afire, heated by desire, racked with a need that had gone seven years without fulfilment.

Sometimes, when in the dead of night she had allowed herself to remember the way they made love, she had wondered whether perhaps she had embroidered his basic expertise into a sexual brilliance that no real man could be expected to match.

But if anything her memory had been deficient. Guy was at once tender and fierce, masterful and loving, dominating and receptive. And he knew exactly what to do to make her gasp and sob, to stoke the fires of her passion until she couldn't open her eyes, couldn't do anything more than brokenly whisper his name, all thought submerged in the mindless currents of pleasure that swirled around her and through her at the skilled touch of his hands and his mouth.

When at last he moved over her Mike opened her eyes, needing to see his face as they joined. With his angular, set features, he looked angry, his lips drawn back from his teeth in something that was almost a snarl, but she wasn't afraid. Slowly, carefully, he eased into her, measured himself in the tight sheath that opened for him, enclosed him, took him home.

'Guy,' Mike whispered, her hips rotating in a sinuous movement.

'No! *Just—stay—still*.'

For long moments they lay joined but unmoving, while both in their various ways fought to control the wildfire passion that threatened to run away with them.

Then he said in a shaken voice, 'God, next time, Mike; it will have to be next time,' and thrust deeply into her.

Together, lost in an enchantment, they strove for the heights, the rapturous melding of emotion and sensation that existed somewhere beyond the ordinary realm of the senses.

Mike discovered it a little before he did. Ripples turned into waves, into breakers that spread from her heated core to her extremities. She cried out, and he said hoarsely, 'Let it go, Mike, let it go; it's all right, I've got you.'

It frightened her, because she was no longer Mike, she was merely feeling, lost to everything but the surge of elemental response, the exhilaration that couldn't be denied. Joined to him in some way even more basic than the physical, she surrendered to his fierce, driving possession, to the heat of his body, the slickness of his skin beneath her fingers, the wild thunder of her heart in her ears, his taste in her mouth.

Her eyes dilated. Pleasure undreamed of tore a muffled gasp from her throat; she shivered as the waves broke over her, and almost immediately he followed, every muscle in his lean body strained in ecstasy, his head flung back as he poured the essence of his masculinity into her.

Mike had forgotten that the aftermath was so satisfying. Guy's weight was heavy on her, yet she wasn't uncomfortable.

This is what I was made for, she thought dreamily, her hands sliding up and down the sleek, taut muscles of his back. This is who I was made for. This man. Guy.

After a long time he moved, ignoring her murmur of protest, and tucked her in beside him, her head on the smooth swell of his shoulder. Mike stretched languorously, and kissed his skin, tasting with delicate greed the salty tang of him.

'Don't do that,' he said.

'Why not?'

'Because the feel of your little tongue on my skin does strange things to me.'

She thought this over. 'Does it?' she said demurely, and kissed him, open-mouthed, taking her time about it.

He said nothing, but she felt the sudden tension in his big body, so she went on exploring, finding the little nub of his nipple beneath the silken overlay of hair. It was tight and hard. First she licked it, then took it into her mouth and suckled, as he had done to her.

'Unless you know what you're doing, you had better stop.' His voice rumbled in his chest.

Mike looked up. Through the tangle of lashes his eyes glittered like the sheen of lamplight on a Spanish blade, and as she lifted her head he shivered.

Mike leaned her cheek on his midriff and looked down his body. Even she knew that most men needed some considerable time to recover from a bout of passion, but it appeared that Guy was an exception.

Smiling, she reached down and touched him, following the pointer of hair down past his waist and on, until she found the satin-steel length of him.

'I think I know what I'm doing,' she said softly.

This time it was slower, smoother, the hard edge of passion transformed to deliberate sensuality, so that Mike was almost pleading with him when at last he slid into her. It took longer to reach that pinnacle of rapture, and the descent was more leisurely, but as she lay almost asleep, his arms locked around her, the heat and potent masculine scent of his body wrapped around her, she realised that neither time had he lost control. She had fallen apart in his arms, sobbed and gasped and pleaded for him never to stop, but he had always been completely in control not only of her responses but of his own.

She was too tired to worry about it then, but it was the first thing she thought of when she woke the next morning, alone in the bed. A note on her bedside table said in bold, angular handwriting,

My heart, I'm sorry but I have a meeting. Do what you want to until ten o'clock. I'll be back then.

It was nine-thirty. With a horrified grimace, Mike cast a disparaging glance around the dark room and hurtled out of the huge bed to pull the curtains back.

Scarcely was that done, and the room flooded with the sun's golden light, than a knock on the door made her dive for the bed and haul the sheet up over her breasts. He was early.

But it was a distinctly feminine voice that called out, 'Guy, where are you?' And it was the heels of a woman's shoes that tapped across the sitting-room, heading unerringly for the bedroom.

CHAPTER EIGHT

A WOMAN walked in through the door, tall and serenely elegant, her beauty and cool patrician air immediately intimidating. At the sight of Mike, crouched against the tumbled pillows, she stopped, arched brows pleating in astonishment.

'Hello,' she said slowly.

Horrified, embarrassed and furious, Mike muttered, 'Hello.'

The stranger smiled. 'Oh, dear, I suppose I should have told him I was coming. I'm Caroline Hammer, and I used to be married to Guy. And you are...?'

'Mike Christopher.' Mike knew that she was being abrupt, but she had been seized by a pang of jealousy so intense that she could barely breathe from the pain of it, let alone talk.

Guy's ex-wife gave a small, sympathetic chuckle. 'This is not in the least embarrassing,' she said firmly. 'If we say it often enough we might even come to believe it. You're a very good friend of Guy's, I assume?'

'We met about seven years ago.' Admiring the other woman's sang-froid, Mike tried hard to emulate it, although she cringed at the thought of the way she must look. However, she wasn't going to have this woman think she was a casual pick-up.

Something moved in Caroline Hammer's green eyes. 'So you're the one,' she breathed, fixing her gaze on Mike as she sat down on the side of the bed. 'I always knew there was someone. He tried damned hard, poor Guy, but I knew. You can always tell, can't you?'

Mike sat up, holding the sheet protectively over her bare breasts. She was angry and mortified, with herself for being caught in such a situation, with Guy for not telling her that his ex-wife still strolled into his bedroom whenever she felt like it, and with the woman sitting opposite her for being so bloody self-confident, and for marrying Guy.

Above all, for marrying Guy.

'Is everything all right now?' Caroline asked, clearly interested. 'Between you and Guy, I mean.'

Mike said stiffly, 'Look, I don't really know what you're talking about...'

Caroline sighed. 'I'm sorry, I know I'm being impertinent and awful, but if you knew how often I've wondered just what you were like, and how impotent I felt about the whole business! It's ironic, you know. I used to think you must be the most beautiful creature in the world, but you're not. Yet Guy couldn't forget you.'

Mike thrust a hand through her hair, pushing it back from her face. She didn't know what on earth to say to this self-assured woman.

'I used to resent you bitterly,' Caroline went on, her voice very soft and almost amused. 'Whenever he looked at me, whenever he made love, he saw you. He's a magnificent lover, isn't he? But somehow, although he was invariably sensitive and wildly exciting, it always seemed mechanical. I mean, he never lost control. Not once! And he was gentle rather than tender. Very bad for the self-esteem, that sort of thing is.'

Mike had to grind her teeth together to stop the hot, angry words from spilling out. She said feverishly, 'Look, I don't think we should be discussing him——'

'Because it makes you jealous?' Caroline Hammer gave her a cool, considering stare. 'You needn't worry; he didn't love me. We had a lot in common, that's all.' Mike didn't move, didn't say anything, but Caroline Hammer nodded wisely. 'No, that wouldn't do for you. You'd want a marriage based on a lot more than affection and sex and the same background. But plenty of marriages are established on much more flimsy grounds than ours, and have been perfectly happy. We had the same interests, we knew the same people, we liked the same sort of things, and I'm as good a hostess as he is a lover. Of course, he only married me because his grandfather more or less told him he wouldn't get the business if he didn't.'

Mike said shakily, 'And you knew that?'

'Oh, yes.' She gave a crooked smile. 'In fact, I gave the old man the idea. He wanted Guy to marry me—he thought I was just the sort of person to make him a good wife. I did too.'

Mike drew a deep breath. She shouldn't be discussing Guy like this, but he had told her so little of himself that she was desperate for knowledge. 'Did either of you know that Guy wasn't in love with you?'

Caroline Hammer smiled sardonically. 'Grandfather Bishop didn't believe that love was much of a basis for marriage. Guy doesn't, either. His parents loved each other, but they couldn't live together, and I think old Forbes chose his wife because she was quiet and obedient and would be a good hostess and mother. He always used to say that it was a very happy marriage. I've often wondered whether Mrs Bishop was quite as happy as he thought.'

Mike looked down at her hands, not long and slender and elegant like the other woman's; hers were more competent, she thought with a faint flash of hysteria. Fine for doing things; not so good for showing off rings.

Which was cattiness pure and simple, because apart from a thin gold wedding-band—Guy's?—Caroline Hammer wasn't wearing any rings.

'Why did you want to marry him?' Mike hadn't intended to ask the question, but it came before she could stop it.

Caroline flushed slightly, but looked Mike straight in the eye. 'Because he was magnificent in bed. Because I was the envy of all my friends. Because he could give me the sort of life I was accustomed to. There were a lot of reasons, none of which had much to do with love, I'm ashamed to say.'

At least she hadn't been hurt too much by that doomed marriage.

Remembering Guy's offhand remark that he had had to make adjustments to win his way to take over the business, Mike said slowly, 'So his grandfather more or less blackmailed Guy into marrying you?'

Caroline's slim shoulders lifted. 'I suppose you could call it that. Guy had always been told he was going to get the business, but the old man said no, not unless he married. He didn't say it had to be me, but he made it quite obvious that it had to be a woman he approved of. Guy defied him and stormed off up to Far Winds; he still refused flatly when he came back. But a couple of months later he gave in.'

The propensity to use blackmail obviously ran in the family. Too much was buzzing around in Mike's brain, but she said incredulously, 'And you were quite happy to marry him even though he didn't love you and you didn't love him?'

Caroline shrugged again. 'I thought that affection and shared interests and a certain amount of lust was enough to base a good marriage on. And for a while it seemed as though everything was going to be all right. He did his best to make me a good husband. I certainly tried to be the sort of wife he needed. But it never really worked, and eventually it just crumbled. There you were in the background, like the skeleton in the cupboard, or the ghost in the bed——'

Mike said brusquely, 'How did you know it was me?'

'I guessed. I mean, I knew there was another woman. Once we had a fight and I asked him why he hadn't married you; he said you were very young, and very unsophisticated. You'd never have been able to cope with the sort of life we led.' She smiled. 'Amusing, isn't it? Because I could—I was brought up to it—yet it didn't help our marriage any. Not that he was unfaithful; he's almost fanatically loyal. But it was a mockery of a marriage, right from the start. After a while we didn't even sleep together. We were married for a couple of years, but I suppose we only lived as man and wife for six months or so.'

Mike was sure her expression didn't alter, but the other woman saw something in her face, because she smiled, almost sympathetically. 'There are different sorts of loyalty, you know. He was loyal to his grandfather. And it probably wouldn't have worked out if he'd lost his head and married you then. Love is desirable, but it's not everything, and sometimes it's just not enough. Ask him about his parents. They almost tore each other apart until finally they just gave up.'

The telephone's shrill summons sounded shockingly abrupt in the quiet, opulent room. Eyes dilating, Mike stared at it.

'You'd better answer it,' Caroline Hammer said with a wry smile. 'It's probably Guy.'

It was, his tone teasing and intimate. 'Good morning,' he said. 'I hated to leave you, but I had an early appointment.'

Mike said stiffly, 'Yes.'

His voice altered, became sharp and hard. 'What's the matter?'

'Nothing. Your w . . . ex-wife is here.'

'*Who*?' She couldn't answer, and he was silent for a moment before saying crisply, 'Put her on.'

Mutely, Mike held out the receiver. With lifted brows and a half-smile Caroline took the handpiece. A faint, expensive perfume, clear and clean and urbane, drifted across Mike's nostrils.

She looked away, painfully conscious of her rumpled hair, and the bed, with its evidence of violent passion still obvious for anyone to see. Caroline was too fastidious to reveal her emotions, but she could be in no doubt as to what had happened in that bed the previous night.

'Oh, we decided to enjoy the flesh-pots for a couple of nights. We anchored here late last night,' Caroline said, laughing. She listened to Guy's imperative voice before replying soothingly, 'No, of course I'm not. Come on, now, Guy, you know me better than that.' She laughed again, a delicious little sound. 'I have got news for you, but I'll tell you later; it's not urgent.'

He answered that at some length and she lifted her lashes so that she was looking at Mike, her green eyes very astute, still wryly amused.

'Yes, I think you may have a point, and because it might have something to do with me I'll do it,' she said, and laughed, and held out the receiver. 'Here, he wants to talk to you.'

Only pride kept Mike's voice steady. 'What do you want?'

'Don't get uptight with me,' he said with crisp emphasis. 'Do as Caroline says. Goodbye.'

She hung up, trying to straighten the whirling confusion in her brain.

'Come on,' Caroline Hammer said briskly. 'Get up and we'll have a game of golf together.'

Mike's jaw dropped. She said faintly, 'You can't possibly want to play golf with me.'

'I do, I do indeed. I'm as curious as hell about you. And face it, even though you resent me, you're curious about me as well, aren't you? If you're going to have any place in Guy's life you'll be seeing me quite often. Although we're no longer married we move in the same circles.'

Mike asked, 'Why did you divorce him?'

'We divorced each other,' the other woman told her readily. 'It was quite amicable. Come on, get up and get going.'

'I can't.' Fleeting colour tinged Mike's cheeks. 'I haven't got any clothes apart from the ones I had on yesterday.'

Caroline Hammer grinned. 'What size are you?'

Mike told her.

'Good. You order some breakfast, and I'll get something for you to wear from the boutique. I'll be back in half an hour. Save some coffee for me.'

Bemused, Mike obeyed her, and, still bemused, showered and washed her hair. When she emerged from the bathroom there was no sign of Caroline, but she could hear movement in the front room. Breakfast, no doubt.

I must be mad, she breathed, as she climbed into yesterday's crumpled trousers and shirt. She hesitated, looking down at the bed, then pulled it carefully back to air before leaving the room.

She was eating a slice of toast when the door opened and Caroline walked back into the room, dangling parcels. 'Good, you haven't done a bunk,' she said cheerfully. 'I thought you might, although, knowing Guy, he's got someone posted at the wharf to make sure you don't get off the island.'

She dropped the parcels on to the sofa and walked across to look at the painting above the fireplace. 'A Blair Doyle, I'll bet. I recognise her style. She has great talent.'

'Yes,' Mike agreed woodenly, wondering, not for the first time, just why she had let this woman bulldoze her.

A crystalline wall seemed to separate her from the rest of the world. While she poured coffee for an affably chatting Caroline she tried to convince herself that it was perfectly normal and modern for an ex-wife and a mistress to sit down in such amity.

Caroline asked her what she did for a living, appeared very interested in her reply, and airily admitted to doing nothing. She discussed a few burning questions of the day with moderation and good sense, and drank coffee with every appearance of enjoyment. Mike wished she had such unsinkable poise.

And then Caroline looked over Mike's shoulder and said, 'Ah, here he is,' and smiled.

Mike's head whipped around. Guy walked in through the door, looking watchful and constrained.

'All right?' he asked curtly.

Caroline got to her feet. 'She seems a bit disassociated,' she said cheerfully over her shoulder as she headed for the door, 'but you can explain. I'll see you around, Mike.'

Not if I see you first, Mike thought, brought to sudden, blazing life by his appearance. Sheer bloody-mindedness made her demand belligerently, 'What about the golf?' to the door as it closed behind Caroline.

'A ruse. To make sure you didn't cut and run. Come on,' Guy said, holding out an imperative hand.

'Where to?'

He looped his fingers around her wrist, pulling her up against him. 'This place is too public. I'm very fond of Caroline now that I'm not married to her, but I don't want to see her beaming at me from behind every damned pot plant. And I've still got meetings—we won't have any time together for the rest of the week. Why the hell did you decide to arrive here early, and throw all my plans completely out? The best thing for you to do is go back to Russell and wait for me there.' He gave her a swift, hard kiss. 'Try to miss me.'

He didn't take her back himself. A keen young man waited down in the foyer, and ferried her across to Russell in a sleek speedboat. Behind his polite, respectful mask, she sensed a prurient interest in her position in Guy's life.

This, of course, was what being a mistress was all about: available when he wanted her, banished to the sidelines when other, more important things needed his attention. At least he hadn't suggested she amuse herself by the pool until he was ready!

Back in her unit she sat down on the sofa and stared out into the garden. The memory of Caroline's artless revelations made her feel sick. She got herself a glass of water, watching her hand tremble with a kind of detached interest.

Strange that her sense of betrayal should be so acute. After all, it had happened seven years ago. Yet the pain was as raw as though only yesterday he had left her and married a woman he didn't love, just to acquire money and power.

But he hadn't loved Mike Christopher, either. It was stupid to feel that he had stripped her of pride and self-esteem. He could only do that if she let him. He had simply behaved like a hard-headed, intelligent, practical businessman, making deals and working out the way to make the most profit from the situation. That was what he was doing now.

Sudden, painful tears blurred the glass in her hand. She set her jaw and drank the water down. Last night had been folly of the highest order; she had allowed Guy's dark magic to persuade her into doing something that now seemed sordid and foolish. Looking around at the cheerful, casually comfortable room, so different from the opulent luxury of Far Winds, it was as though she had walked out from a mist of ensorcellment, just as happened in the old fairy-tales.

Except, she thought with a contemptuous half-smile, that she had been an agent in her own destruction. She couldn't blame Guy for too much; she had gone very willingly down that enigmatic and perilous path of the senses.

Shame heated her skin as she remembered some of the things that she had done the night before, the things she had let him do. Yes, she had been as wild and passionate as he, lost in a white-hot delirium where the only thing that mattered was the man who touched her with such consuming need.

That was last night. This was today.

Blindly, she got to her feet and wandered across to the window.

She would cut her losses. He might want to get her out of his system as painlessly as possible, but she had better things to do with her life than let him use her like that.

At least she no longer remembered him with a romantic haze; she knew now exactly what sort of man he was. If she'd been a little more worldly seven years ago she'd have realised that when he had blackmailed her into going out to dinner he had been behaving according

to his nature. Or perhaps, she thought, according to the
way he'd been brought up. His grandfather sounded like
a chauvinistic old villain. No wonder Guy was hard and
manipulative.

She'd go back to Auckland. Now.

He knew where she lived, so she was only gaining time,
but she needed that time desperately to reassemble her
defences. Just before lunch she set out on the three-and-
a-half-hour journey to Auckland, driving with such
concentration that for that time she almost forgot her
pain.

He was waiting when she drove into the motor court
of her apartments.

Mike's stomach cramped. She knew that he noticed
her shock—when did anything escape those damned
perceptive eyes?—but with head held high she got out
of her car.

Behind him stood another man. A minion, Mike decided, dismissing him after a quick glance.

'Hello, Mike,' Guy said. 'Did you have a good trip
down?'

Mike said thinly, 'What are you doing here?'

His smile, narrow as a sword-blade, told her how
furious he was. 'Surely you expected me?' He held out
a hand for her keys.

For a fleeting moment Mike thought of resistance, but
one quick glance at the dark face above her decided her
against such a futile act. Still smiling, Guy took the keys
from her hand and tossed them over her head to the
second man.

'What the hell do you think you're doing?' she said
in a voice that was both angry and afraid.

'Kidnapping you, darling. Are you going to come
quietly, or do I have to push you into my car?'

He didn't wait for an answer. Before she had time to
scream, or kick, or do any of the things she thought of
later, he had bustled her into the passenger seat, locked
the door on her, and was walking around the front of
the car with a swift, lithe purposefulness that chilled her

even as she tried desperately to open her door.
Unfortunately the man she had so easily discounted was
on guard. He wasn't looking at her; he was dumping
the suitcase he'd taken from her car on to the seat behind
her, but she knew that he was there to make sure she
couldn't get out. She sent him a glowering, hate-filled
glare. By that time Guy was already in the driver's seat.

'I'll never forgive you for this,' she said wrathfully.

He started the engine. 'What else can I do?' he said
as he eased the big car out on to the street. His voice
was reasonable, but she sensed implacable determination behind the calm words, and knew that she was
not going to escape. 'You keep running away.'

'How did you know I'd gone? I thought you were in
a meeting.'

'I was. But I decided to give the conference a miss for
a couple of days, so I rang you. Only to have your
landlady tell me that you'd packed up and gone.
Naturally, I followed you.'

'I won't be harassed like this!'

He shrugged. 'You'll do as you're told,' he said indifferently. 'I'm sick of chasing you and losing you.
We're going to get this finished with once and for all.'

His face revealed an inexorable resolve that frustrated
her into foolish bravado. She said huskily, 'So kidnapping as well as blackmailing runs in your family. You
could damned well end up in gaol.'

'Just see it as an indication of how necessary I feel
this to be,' he said coolly.

Any loss of control handed him an automatic advantage, and Mike wasn't going to do that. She didn't
know what he planned to do, whether talking was all he
had in mind. Probably not, she thought, trying to whip
up a righteous fury. Unfortunately it was sabotaged by
a secret, involuntary excitement that heated her limbs
and ran slow and sweet as syrup through her veins.

He was unscrupulous enough to use every bit of
leverage he could, and he knew damned well that
physically she had no defences against him.

In a few minutes he drove into a garage beneath a building Mike recognised. Why on earth had he brought her to his office? Briefly she toyed with the idea of refusing to get out, of making him drag her from the car, but she knew him well enough to realise that he would do that if he had to. And she was afraid of her own responses. She was too physically aware of him, her body and reactions too treacherous to be trusted.

So she stalked ahead of him, her back stiff with resentment, into a lift. It rose rapidly and silently right to the top, where they emerged at a roof garden. And there was their destination. One side of the garden had been transformed into a helipad, and on it, rotors whirring, waited a shiny silver helicopter.

'Where are we going?' she demanded, stopping.

His hand on her arm was irresistible, but just in case she didn't get the message he said amiably, 'The pilot isn't going to worry if I pick you up and carry you on board. He'll think it's a lovers' tiff. Or even that I'm being romantic.'

'Not if I'm kicking and screaming and pulling your hair,' she said between her teeth.

'Stop sulking,' he returned, urging her towards the machine.

'I am not sulking. I am absolutely furious. How dare you behave like this? Who the hell do you think you are——?'

'I'm a man who's sick and tired of trying to persuade his woman to listen to him,' he said brutally. 'If you don't like it, blame yourself, lady.'

'I have every right to refuse to go with you, damn you!'

'Shut up,' he said, bored. 'We'll discuss things when we've reached the island.'

'What island?'

'My island.' He looked down at her, his expression hard to define. 'Once we're there nobody will be able to interfere.'

Simmering with frustrated fury, Mike let herself be boosted into the cabin and belted in. She refused to look anywhere but out of the side-window as they rose into the air, staring savagely down at the business centre of the city. It wasn't yet sunset but the air had that sated, heavy feel to it that the end of the day often brought, as though it longed for the cool sweetness of dusk.

Within minutes they were flying over the Hauraki Gulf, that much bigger version of the Bay of Islands, its vast expanse sheltered from the mighty Pacific Ocean by a whole string of islands ranging in size from the sixty-mile length of Great Barrier to elegant little jewels closer to the city.

Mike looked back at Auckland's sprawl, thousands of houses set in tree-lined streets, with more trees in each backyard. It was home now, she realised. Not home as the Bay of Islands had been, not the centre of her universe, but home where her heart rested.

Because of course she loved Guy. She had always known it; she had just refused to admit it, because it made her seem such a wimp, loving a man who saw her as nothing more than an irritant, a burr under his saddle, a woman he wanted to make love to so that eventually he wouldn't want her any more.

He was treating her like medicine, a vaccine, whereas she, bewitched by some dark enchantment, was irrevocably bound to him. She had loved him when she first met him, she had loved him for the seven long years of his absence in her life, and she loved him now.

She was probably like her mother; she'd love him until she died.

It hadn't done anything for Linda, that lifelong love, and it certainly wasn't doing anything for her. Guy wanted her with a hunger that excited her and appalled her, because she felt it too, that feral wildness in the blood, that overwhelming need to take him and never let him go. But he didn't love her. Perhaps he couldn't love.

Nothing had changed. Oh, she was more sophisticated now than she had been when she was twenty, but he was even harder than he had been then, a man who would marry a woman for profit, to retain his grip on power.

He was going to use his hold on her, his sexual power over her, to persuade her into resuming their affair. But he would be helped by that other hold he didn't know about, her fierce, hopeless love. Gritting her teeth, she presented him with her rigid profile.

She had two choices, the same two dreary choices. She could become his mistress, and live in a poisoned paradise for as long as it took for him to get her out of his system, or she could refuse him.

She didn't fool herself that that would be easy. He had no scruples where she was concerned; witness this kidnapping!

But the alternative was frightening, far too terrifying even to consider. For when it finished, as it inevitably would, he'd go on his way and she'd be left with nothing but empty memories to sustain her emotions for the rest of her life.

Common sense told her that eventually she would forget him, eventually she would find a man she could respect, a man who would respect her. But on some deep instinctual level she knew that there would never be another man like Guy. Somehow he had branded her with the imprint of his personality.

She would have to match him, meet his strength with hers, use whatever weapons she could to fight the spell he had cast over her.

Their destination was a tree-clad dot of land barely more than five acres in extent, tucked inconspicuously between Kawau Island and the mainland. A jetty with a shed on it ran out from the base of a low rocky cliff, and a track wound towards the house that crouched among trees and shrubs. It had the potent appeal of all islands, a romantic remoteness. Mike looked down on a white-painted flagstaff at one side of the house, a tennis court on the other, and a beach the colour of apricots out in front. Another house sprawled beside a tiny cove where the sand glowed golden in the westering rays of the sun.

The helicopter landed with delicate precision on the green grass. Guy and the pilot began to unload several boxes of supplies. Mike strode away across the newly mown grass.

'Not going to help?' Guy said, and in the gathering dusk his teeth gleamed for an instant.

'This is your idea,' she said offhandedly. 'You do the work.'

And stood staring resolutely out to sea until the helicopter rose like an ungainly dragonfly and flew away. When the whump-whump-whump of the rotors had died down and there was no sound but the gentle hush of the waves on the beach, Guy came across the grass towards her.

He laughed softly. 'I keep discovering hitherto unrevealed aspects of your character.'

'You don't know me at all.'

'I know you're good in bed,' he mocked.

'And that's all that counts to you,' she returned, pain making her vicious.

'You don't know me at all well, either,' he said blandly. 'Come on, let's go inside before it gets too dark to see.'

The house wasn't big, and it wasn't particularly opulent, but the furnishings were luxurious and comfortable. Mike preceded him into a large tiled sitting-room.

'The light switches are to your left,' he said. 'The bedroom and bathroom are straight ahead. Don't try to run away; there's nowhere to go but the caretaker's house, and he won't help you.' His voice hardened. 'This is my house, my island, my refuge. You're here until I decide to let you go.'

Mike turned the lights on, looking around with some appreciation in spite of her fury and desolation. Now that she was here, she was almost shivering with tension.

He looked suddenly big and forbidding and frightening, effortlessly dominating the large room with his powerful presence.

Guy came back, glanced at her still standing irresolute in the centre of the room, then moved around the little kitchen, putting away groceries in a shocking parody of domesticity. With dilated eyes Mike watched him. He looked untamed, walking with a lithe grace that daunted as well as agitated her. She was alone on the island with him; she wasn't strong enough to prevent him from doing whatever he wanted to.

Stop it, she commanded her brain. This is *Guy*, not some unknown rapist.

Yet he had the power to harm her more than any pervert, because she loved him.

Love was so unfair. You couldn't love to order and it didn't allow for half-measures; it was a simple matter of tossing your heart over and following where it landed. Sheer self-preservation should prevent such recklessness.

It made her so vulnerable. Her whole being was exposed and unprotected. He could hurt her so much, and she could do nothing, because he didn't love her; his emotions were safely protected.

'What is it?' he asked.

Mike jumped. He had come across the room and she hadn't noticed.

With ungentle hands he turned her to face him, his expression rigidly controlled. 'Don't flinch away from me,' he said grimly. 'I will never hurt you, Mike. Why the sad little look?'

'I don't want to be here.'

'I know you don't, but we need this time together. I'd planned for us to have next week alone at Far Winds—but you queered that by arriving early.'

'I suppose I should be flattered that you're prepared to give up valuable time with your executives,' she said, holding herself stiffly erect and away from the too attractive lure of his arms. 'Unless the esoteric lure of kidnapping is more important to you than boring business meetings.'

'Damn my executives.' His voice, the angular lines of his face, were inflexible. 'And I don't find business meetings boring. However, given a choice between business meetings and you, I'll take you every time. Why don't you unpack? I'll get dinner ready.'

'I'm going to take a shower,' she said acidly.

He gave her a slow, ironic smile. 'Your suitcase is in the bedroom. I'll see you in half an hour.'

It was an order. Mike turned and went through the door and into the hall, wondering why she should choose now to feel so afraid.

The room was the main bedroom, and for a moment she toyed with the idea of finding herself another one, but she didn't. It would be better to save her energy for the important battles, she thought sardonically.

A small bathroom, completely tiled in marble, led off the room. Brows drawing together, Mike snatched a pair of trousers and a shirt from her suitcase and went into the bathroom. Was it only last night that they had made love on Far Winds? It seemed an aeon ago, separated by far more than the hundred and fifty miles and twenty-four hours.

She took as long as she dared, walking back into the sitting-room with her head held high and an arrogant, touch-me-not look. Guy looked up as she came in, but although she glared at him defiantly he said merely, 'What would you like to drink?'

'Nothing,' she said, irritated by his imperturbable *savoir-faire*. 'Guy, this is ridiculous! Why did you bring me here?'

He lifted his brows, smiling, yet not amused. 'I've told you why.'

'Then for God's sake get on and talk!'

'I should have known that you'd run,' he said coolly, 'as you did the first time we made love. You seemed shocked, almost shattered by what happened last night.'

She looked away. 'I—it was—I lost control.'

'I noticed.' He was smiling, although his eyes were very keen as they searched her face. 'Why does that embarrass you? That's what you're supposed to do when you make love. Are you ashamed of it?'

Yes, when he so obviously hadn't. 'No,' she said in a stifled voice. 'I just think it's not a good idea. I'm not cut out to be a mistress.' Too possessive; too demanding. She didn't want the crumbs of his life; she wanted it all.

'So you ran. Is that how you deal with your life, Mike? Sweep it under the carpet, run away from it?'

'No more so than anybody else.' She collapsed into a chair and said wearily, 'This is not going to work.'

'You haven't given it a chance.'

How could she tell him that she loved him, that she had never stopped loving him, and that to be his mistress, to watch and wait like Caroline for him to lose control, would kill her?

To him other things were much more important than love—the business, his social standing, money, power. Caroline might not have been intending to cause trouble, but her candid revelations had confirmed Mike's instinctive understanding of Guy's character.

'Why did you run?' His voice was smooth and pleasant, but she discerned an inexorable will in his tone.

Harshly, she explained, 'I need a little more from a man than lust. Tell me, how long did you think we'd go on like this? Until you found another suitable woman to marry?'

He said nothing, but his mouth compressed and a thin white line appeared around it.

She drew a ragged breath and went on, 'I wonder if you know how bloody insulting you are. You wouldn't marry me last time because I wasn't suitable, but I was perfectly all right to take to bed. You caved in when your horrible old grandfather——'

He said roughly, 'You and Caroline must have had an interesting conversation. It sounds as though she paid me back for a few old grievances. Did she tell you that my grandfather gave her a million dollars to marry me?'

'You should have been very happy,' she flung back. 'You have so much in common—all of you. Money and power before everything!'

He looked at her with such black fury that she flinched back. 'I'm not going to hit you,' he said savagely. 'I have better things to do with you than that. Come on, eat something. You must be hungry.'

Food was the last thing she wanted, but she ate the ham salad he had made nevertheless. And she did feel better for it.

When the dishes were in the washer and they were sitting with coffee, she said abruptly, 'You're quite ruthless, aren't you, when it comes to getting what you want?'

'When the thing I want is you, yes.'

She laughed with bitter emphasis. 'Oh, yes, you wanted me so much that you sent me away.'

'Is that why you ran?' he asked incredulously.

Mike bit her lip, furious with herself for letting that slip. 'Partly,' she admitted, grudging him even that small understanding.

'I sent you away because you'd made it obvious you didn't want to be the butt of everyone's attention.' He set his cup down and got up to walk across to the window, thrusting his hands into his pockets. Staring out at the lights of the mainland, he said between his teeth, 'And because with you off Far Winds I thought I might be able to concentrate on something more than how I came apart in your arms last night.'

Mike said doggedly, 'I don't want to be your mistress.'

'I thought we were lovers,' he countered, still with his back to her.

Mike's gaze followed the width of his shoulders, remembering how they had felt under her hands, the muscles hard and tense beneath skin like finest glove-leather, the erotic, overwhelming sensation of being captive by his much greater strength, and the knowledge that he would never use that strength against her.

She said with painful honesty, 'Guy, it won't work, because I need more than that.'

He shrugged. 'All right. Marry me.'

Mike stared at him, her mouth falling foolishly open. Just as he turned to face her, she realised he'd been watching her in the dark reflective glass.

He laughed cynically. 'No, it hadn't even occurred to you, had it?'

'You've already had one loveless marriage,' she said over the sound of her shattering heart. 'Don't you think that's enough for a lifetime, or are you planning to make a habit of it? I'm not Caroline; I haven't anything that will help your ambitions——'

'Mike, don't,' he said raggedly. 'Would it be so hard to love me?'

Mike's mouth was dry, her skin stretched tightly over her bones. In a tired voice she asked, 'Why do you want me to love you? Isn't it enough that I can't bloody well stay away from you, that every time I let you talk me into bed because I can't resist you? Do you have to degrade me even further?'

'I'm sorry you think loving me is such a degradation,' he said savagely, 'because I want you to be as totally consumed by me as I am by you. Damn it, Mike, do you think I'd behave like this for any other reason than that I'm driven to it? With you I've always been a coward, and I despise myself for it. I married Caroline because I was afraid of what I felt for you, so I ran away from it, hurting her and hurting you. I don't normally kidnap women; I don't normally behave like something Neanderthal with more testosterone than brains!' He gave a harsh, humourless laugh. 'Believe it or not, usually I conduct my affairs like any other decent citizen! But these last seven years have been pure hell, and when you ran this morning I thought, I can't deal with the loneliness, the knowledge that my own stupidity has ruined the best thing that ever happened to me. I thought you might be getting ready to run even further than Auckland. There was no choice; I had to leave my executives to their own devices and follow you.'

Mike ran a hand through her hair, fighting a hope so forlorn that she couldn't articulate it. 'What are you saying?' she demanded, staring at him.

He took a deep, painful breath, but didn't move. 'I'm saying that I love you. I've loved you for seven years. That first time—I followed you up to Far Winds to ask you to marry me, but you were gone, and I couldn't find you.'

Completely at a loss, Mike stared at him.

He was watching her with something like desperation sharpening the angular framework of his face. 'Almost immediately afterwards my grandfather had a heart attack, and he made it more than obvious that he wanted me to marry Caroline. So I did, and tried to make it work. I short-changed Caroline, short-changed my grandfather, short-changed you. It didn't take me long to realise what I'd done, and regret it bitterly.'

Mike shook her head and said hopelessly, 'It won't work. I know the sort of life you lead ...'

Moving swiftly, he came over and knelt before her, taking her small, cold hands in his. 'Can't we make it work? Mike, I've had seven years without you, seven long, barren years. I need you, more than I've ever needed anyone in my life before, and you need me too, darling, I know you do. If I have to, if it's necessary, I'll beg.'

'You suggested we have an affair,' she said desperately, lowering her lashes so that the burning blue of his gaze couldn't laser through her will-power. 'You said nothing about marriage.'

'You were the one who talked about an affair; you were the one who didn't want to consider marriage. I wasn't going to frighten you away, but, believe me, I wanted you any way I could get you.' He hesitated, then his hands tightened painfully around hers and he said awkwardly, 'Mike, marry me, please. I'll do my best to make you happy.'

The simple plea touched her heart. She glowered at him. 'All you had to say, you idiot, was that you love me! You don't need to *make* me love you; I've loved you ever since I saw you!'

'Mike?' He got abruptly to his feet, pulling her with him, and stared at her, reading her eyes, his own brilliant and intent.

She glared back at him, knowing that her expression told him everything, exulting in her freedom to reveal her emotions. Renewed confidence brought a challenging sparkle to her eyes, an excitement that manifested itself in the rich curve of her mouth.

He said something short and succinct and prayerful, then swept her into his arms and kissed her with an all-consuming passion.

Hours later she lay on top of him, her cheek pressed against his heart. Their bodies were lax and satisfied, yet nothing could have been more different from the satiation Mike had once hoped for so fervently. She knew now that they would never be so familiar with this heart-catching passion that desire became routine.

'I love you,' she said into his throat, listening to his heart slowly regulate itself.

'In spite of the massive shambles I made of our lives?'

'You speak for yourself,' she murmured. 'You made a shambles of your life. I went away and did very well for myself.'

Laughter lifted his chest. 'What are you planning to do about your business?'

'Keep going,' she said. 'I enjoy it. I've got a very good woman working for me who can manage it if we have to travel. While you're terrifying your executives I'll spend a lot of time checking out the latest in computers.'

'Sounds the perfect life. I won't be travelling much. I wasted seven years of our life together; I want to spend as much time as possible with you,' he said. 'Incidentally, you don't have to worry about Caroline. We are good friends—it was all we ever were, really—and she's married to a man she's very much in love with.'

'Just as well. When she was talking about you I wanted to slap her senseless,' she said fiercely. 'I feel possessive and demanding and very uncompromising where you're concerned. Very unliberated and unmodern.'

'Good. Because I look at you and all sorts of extremely primitive and barbaric emotions take over.'

'I suppose modern businessmen are the equivalent of the old pirate barons,' she said with satisfaction.

He laughed. 'In spite of appearances to the contrary, I do have ethics,' he told her. 'Will you enjoy living with me, my heart? I don't want you to turn into a social butterfly, but there will be times when we have to entertain.'

Still tender from his kisses, her mouth curled into a smile. 'Times when we want to entertain, I hope, too,' she said. 'Don't worry. We'll cope. After all, when you love each other, that's what you do, isn't it? Compromise and cope.'

'Yes,' he said, his voice heavy with contentment. 'That's what you do.'

Mike yawned. Instantly he lifted her free and tucked her into bed beside him. 'Go to sleep, darling,' he said.

Her last thoughts before she drifted off were happy. The specious glamour of an island enchantment had been deepened, intensified, irradiated by love, a love that had been tempered by time, a love that was going to last.

IT'S FREE! IT'S FUN! ENTER THE

☆ "*Hooray for* ☆
☆ *Hollywood*" ☆

SWEEPSTAKES!

We're giving away prizes to celebrate the screening of four new romance movies on CBS TV this fall! Look for the movies on four Sunday afternoons in October. And be sure to return your Official Entry Coupons to try for a fabulous **vacation in Hollywood!**

 If you're the Grand Prize winner we'll fly you and your companion to Los Angeles for a 7-day/6-night vacation you'll never forget!

 You'll stay at the luxurious Regent Beverly Wilshire Hotel,* a prime location for celebrity spotting!

 You'll have time to visit Universal Studios,* stroll the Hollywood Walk of Fame, check out celebrities' foot-prints at Mann's Chinese Theater, ride a trolley to see the homes of the stars, and more!

 The prize includes a rental car for 7 days and $1,000.00 pocket money!

Someone's going to win this fabulous prize, and it might just be you! Remember, the more times you enter, the better your chances of winning!

> **ALSO**⁺ Five hundred entrants will each receive SUNGLASSES OF THE STARS! Don't miss out. ENTER TODAY!

The proprietors of the trademark are not associated with this promotion.

"HOORAY FOR HOLLYWOOD" SWEEPSTAKES

HERE'S HOW THE SWEEPSTAKES WORKS

OFFICIAL RULES — NO PURCHASE NECESSARY

To enter, complete an Official Entry Form or hand print on a 3" x 5" card the words "HOORAY FOR HOLLYWOOD", your name and address and mail your entry in the pre-addressed envelope (if provided) or to: "Hooray for Hollywood" Sweepstakes, P.O. Box 9076, Buffalo, NY 14269-9076 or "Hooray for Hollywood" Sweepstakes, P.O. Box 637, Fort Erie, Ontario L2A 5X3. Entries must be sent via First Class Mail and be received no later than 12/31/94. No liability is assumed for lost, late or misdirected mail.

Winners will be selected in random drawings to be conducted no later than January 31, 1995 from all eligible entries received.

Grand Prize: A 7-day/6-night trip for 2 to Los Angeles, CA including round trip air transportation from commercial airport nearest winner's residence, accommodations at the Regent Beverly Wilshire Hotel, free rental car, and $1,000 spending money. (Approximate prize value which will vary dependent upon winner's residence: $5,400.00 U.S.); 500 Second Prizes: A pair of "Hollywood Star" sunglasses (prize value: $9.95 U.S. each). Winner selection is under the supervision of D.L. Blair, Inc., an independent judging organization, whose decisions are final. Grand Prize travelers must sign and return a release of liability prior to traveling. Trip must be taken by 2/1/96 and is subject to airline schedules and accommodations availability.

Sweepstakes offer is open to residents of the U.S. (except Puerto Rico) and Canada who are 18 years of age or older, except employees and immediate family members of Harlequin Enterprises, Ltd., its affiliates, subsidiaries, and all agencies, entities or persons connected with the use, marketing or conduct of this sweepstakes. All federal, state, provincial, municipal and local laws apply. Offer void wherever prohibited by law. Taxes and/or duties are the sole responsibility of the winners. Any litigation within the province of Quebec respecting the conduct and awarding of prizes may be submitted to the Regie des loteries et courses du Quebec. All prizes will be awarded; winners will be notified by mail. No substitution of prizes are permitted. Odds of winning are dependent upon the number of eligible entries received.

Potential grand prize winner must sign and return an Affidavit of Eligibility within 30 days of notification. In the event of non-compliance within this time period, prize may be awarded to an alternate winner. Prize notification returned as undeliverable may result in the awarding of prize to an alternate winner. By acceptance of their prize, winners consent to use of their names, photographs, or likenesses for purpose of advertising, trade and promotion on behalf of Harlequin Enterprises, Ltd., without further compensation unless prohibited by law. A Canadian winner must correctly answer an arithmetical skill-testing question in order to be awarded the prize.

For a list of winners (available after 2/28/95), send a separate stamped, self-addressed envelope to: Hooray for Hollywood Sweepstakes 3252 Winners, P.O. Box 4200, Blair, NE 68009.

CBSRLS

OFFICIAL ENTRY COUPON

"Hooray for Hollywood"
SWEEPSTAKES!

Yes, I'd love to win the Grand Prize — a vacation in Hollywood — or one of 500 pairs of "sunglasses of the stars"! Please enter me in the sweepstakes!

This entry must be received by December 31, 1994.
Winners will be notified by January 31, 1995.

Name _____

Address _____ Apt. _____

City _____

State/Prov. _____ Zip/Postal Code _____

Daytime phone number _____
(area code)

Mail all entries to: Hooray for Hollywood Sweepstakes,
P.O. Box 9076, Buffalo, NY 14269-9076.
In Canada, mail to: Hooray for Hollywood Sweepstakes,
P.O. Box 637, Fort Erie, ON L2A 5X3.

KCH

OFFICIAL ENTRY COUPON

"Hooray for Hollywood"
SWEEPSTAKES!

Yes, I'd love to win the Grand Prize — a vacation in Hollywood — or one of 500 pairs of "sunglasses of the stars"! Please enter me in the sweepstakes!

This entry must be received by December 31, 1994.
Winners will be notified by January 31, 1995.

Name _____

Address _____ Apt. _____

City _____

State/Prov. _____ Zip/Postal Code _____

Daytime phone number _____
(area code)

Mail all entries to: Hooray for Hollywood Sweepstakes,
P.O. Box 9076, Buffalo, NY 14269-9076.
In Canada, mail to: Hooray for Hollywood Sweepstakes,
P.O. Box 637, Fort Erie, ON L2A 5X3.

KCH